THE SPEAR
OF
DESTINY II
The Journey Continues

Published by Marshall Enterprises
USA
Marshall Enterprises is committed to excellence in the entertainment industry.

Book design copyright © 2019 by Dianne Marshall. All rights reserved.
Cover design by
Dianne Marshall
Interior design by
Jon Anthony Marshall

Published in the United States of America

ISBN: 978-1-7361278-1-0
1. Fiction / General Action Adventure
2. Fiction / Christian / General
20.17.19

DEDICATION

The Spear of Destiny II is dedicated to all of the Followers of the Way and their journey to spread the "good news"; a journey that began 2,000 years ago and continues to this day.

A salute goes out to all who fight the good fight and come to the aid of those who suffer needlessly at the hands of others.

Dianne Marshall and Jon Anthony

FOREWORD

THE SPEAR OF DESTINY II

The sequel to the novel

"THE SPEAR OF DESTINY"

"A fictional tale placed in a biblical setting that all Christians will find familiar and be able to relate to... but is it actually fiction? Those blessed with both faith and the eyes to see will find this book a very plausible explanation to the origins of the world in which we now live and walk. Perhaps the spear lives on in each of us chosen to confront and conquer the evil."

John Miranda,
Political Analyst & Freelance Journalist, Former, US Navy & US National Swimming Team

CONTENTS

PREFACE

No one knows for sure whether there ever "was" or whether there "is" such an item as the Spear of Destiny that wielded a supernatural power because it speared the side of Christ. There are only contradicting myths and legends.

The fact that after all these years, the search for the Spear was still an obsession for many is what peaked my curiosity to ask the question, *"What happened to create such a legend and mystic pursuit that has lasted all these years?"*

In my quest for the truth, I noticed a legendary trend that stood out like a sore thumb. One that replaced the crucifixion along with the persecution and torturous deaths of the first followers of Christ, the *Followers of the Way,* with that of a magical spear that gave the one who wielded it the power to rule the world. With one little curse - once the spear leaves the possession of the one who wields it, that individual dies within a matter of days.

That is quite a spin on Isaiah's prophecy that not one of his bones shall be broken. I thought about that long, deep and hard.

That being said, I decided to write my own story of the spear, and place the focus on the trials and persecutions of the first Followers of the Way based on historical timelines, guided by the little nuggets of truth that won't go away no matter how hard they are forced to be hidden.

In so doing the book took on its own revelation. Longinus would learn that the power of the spear is not in the spear itself, but in the power of the blood shed by the Nazarene named Jesus on the cross at Golgotha. It was in writing the sequel that I began to see the beginning of the legend and myths of the spear.

Could it be that the historic truth of Jesus the Christ was passed along in a grail like code pointing to the blood on the spear as a symbolic milestone for all who have eyes to see and ears to hear? For the message of the first Followers was and still is that salvation lies within the power of the blood and those who search and find it shall have everlasting life, those who do not shall taste of death at the end of days.

Could it be so simple? Could the hunt for the spear be the hunt for the true message of the Followers of the Way? It is written that all those who seek shall find it. But, always lurking in the shadows are the powers of evil principalities who seek to destroy all who dare to call on the power of the blood of Jesus the Christ. For evil knows that those that find it shall be granted the strength to stand against the evil ones and have access to the full armor of God, which includes the power to wield the mighty sword (spear?) of the Lord, which is the Word of God. (Ephesians 6:11-24)

The Spear of Destiny II, portrays this message for those who have eyes to see and ears to hear. It shows how the demonic powers enter in to kill, steal and destroy. Not in the flesh but through possession of the flesh and all manner of sorcery.

> "For we wrestle not against flesh and blood, but against principalities, against powers, against the rulers of the darkness of this world, against spiritual wickedness in high places,"
> - Ephesians 6:12 (KJV)

What we know for certain is that after the death, burial, and resurrection of the Nazarene named Jesus, all hell broke loose and the ruling powers wanted those who followed him snuffed out and everything HE said, did, and taught along with it. That is the focus of this book and the message I hope the reader takes with them to ponder.

Today we are left with a few fragments of accurate truth while the rest of the history goes untold as though Mary Magdalene suddenly dropped off the face of the earth along with Longinus and the entire lineage of David. It is my hope that the reader find this folk lore fantasy, fitted around historic timelines, as precious as the stories of King Arthur's Court of the Round Table, or Joan of Arc, which both did indeed exist.

Since its very beginning, there has never been a time throughout the history of the world when someone, somewhere on earth was not being mocked, persecuted, tortured or killed for their faith. One thing is certain, a power greater than all the powers in the world combined has kept the true message of the first Followers of the Way alive and those against it have not been able to snuff it out.

That, in and of itself, is a profound mystery.

Dianne Marshall

INTRODUCTION

The story of "The Spear of Destiny" continues...

In the first book, "The Spear of Destiny", the Centurion Longinus, who pierced the side of the Nazarene, later experienced haunting visions from the blood on his spear. Tormented by his visions, he sought help through Mary Magdalene, a woman who was at the crucifixion. His Roman stoic and human stubbornness made it hard for him to listen to what she had to say and instead, believed his destiny was cursed.

Eventually, Mary Magdalene took on the challenge to mentor Longinus and finally cut through his Roman veneer and into his heart. Through her patience and tolerance, Longinus learned he was chosen to fulfill the prophecy that not a one of his bones shall be broken.

He soon discovered the blood on the spear had great power and so did an evil sorcerer known as the Old Man who would stop at nothing to possess it.

Early in the journey, Longinus was hunted down by Romans and one of their hires, a bulked out bounty hunter named Khalid, who had a massive guard dog that looked like a lion and was just as fierce when it came to protecting his master.

After many action packed events, and a sudden change of heart, the bounty hunter joined his mission to help Mary Magdalene and the Followers of the Way to the South of Gaul.

Later, after a series of adventures, Longinus and Khalid left Gaul to help Followers of the Way in Cappadocia.

As time passed, Longinus did not age as everyone else. His ageless persona, coupled with heroic acts of protecting Followers, and countless victories against Roman soldiers gave rise to his increased reputation and fame as one who cannot be killed and does not age. Rome now referred to him as the Enigma.

At the close of the first book, Longinus had just left Mary Magdalene after visiting her at the South of Gaul to find answers to his problems. There was one thing he did not do well and that was his own soul searching. Having faith that something existed that he could not see, touch or fight with his spear, was difficult for him. He did better communicating with people he could see, feel and speak to.

He was of the nature that even when he made great strides forward in faith, he was easy to slide back into his old way of thinking. Whenever he did so, he was more confused than ever.

Our story begins with a refreshing of the last events that lead into this powerful saga *The Spear of Destiny II: The Journey Continues...*

THE HEAD OF THE SPEAR

The year is 63 AD. Throughout the Roman Empire and their conquered territories, Roman soldiers have mercilessly carried out death commands to all followers of the teachings of a Nazarene named Jesus who was put to death by crucifixion in 32 AD.

Since that time, a succession of Caesars have continued to dictate that no one be allowed to follow the teachings of "the way" and those who do were to be subject to persecution and death. Yet, in spite of the decrees, people taught and followed the way of the Nazarene, and their numbers continued to increase.

The hero of our story, Longinus, is the Roman Centurion who pierced the side of the Nazarene with his spear to make sure he was dead. Since that day, Longinus had experienced confusion, agony, and turmoil trying to accept and follow the will of a God different than all he had known in Rome.

It was on the day of the crucifixion that Longinus first met Mary Magdalene and as fate would have it; her influence changed his life forever. After many dramatic events, he chose to protect and provide refuge for all those who follow the way. As time passed he befriended a bounty hunter who at first had sought the price on Longinus's head. Over time, they recruited a band of men to help provide refuge and protection for the followers of the way in a village in Cappadocia.

The village was special in that it had underground passages with secret entrances beneath mythical looking rock chimneys. They equipped these with food and supplies and used them to hide followers from Romans and marauders invading the village which had become a home to many followers and teachers of the way of the Nazarene, named Jesus.

Our story begins at the end of the first book, The Spear of Destiny, where Longinus had left the place of Mary Magdalene near Villalata in the South of Gaul. It had been almost 27 years since he last saw her face. He longed not only to see her, but to ask things he dared not write in a letter regarding the massive killings in the Circus Maximus at the hands of Nero. When he arrived, he realized how much she had aged and he had not.

He spoke of Nero's endless slaughter of followers in the Circus Maximus and his anger at being unable to stop it; he felt his mission was a relentless failure. His attitude for fighting for those who could not fight for themselves had soured. He now perceived their meekness as cowardly and told her it was no wonder Nero picked them off like flies for they never even tried to fight back.

Perhaps it was his weariness from endless battles, coupled with his anger at Nero that skewed his view of the followers as cowards who *would* not fight rather than *could* not fight. Regardless, he selfishly complained that he was fighting in vain, for no matter what he did, Rome continued their evil persecutions, and mass murdering, so what was the point in any of it?

Mary was not at all pleased with Longinus's tale of woe and pointed out, as only Mary could, how it took more courage to hold to their faith, knowing they would be tortured and slaughtered for it than it did to fight with a sword.

After much counseling, and being scolded for going to her for answers instead of going to God, he realized that Mary was right about his self-centered tales of woe and his stubbornness in choosing to take his burdens to her. When he departed, Mary gave him several scrolls to take back to the followers of the way.

After traveling two days on horseback toward Cappadocia, Longinus stopped to make camp. Hungry from his long journey, he rummaged through his haversack for something to eat. Taking some jerky and bread, he curiously looked at the scrolls. He took one out and sat down against a tree where the sun was yet visible and began to skim through it reading here and there as he ate. Suddenly he came to some words that caught his attention. He sat up straight and read it again out loud.

"Peter seeing the disciple saith to Jesus, Lord, and what shall this one do? Jesus saith unto him, if I will that this one tarry till I come, what is that to thee? Follow thou me. Then went this saying abroad among the brethren, that that disciple should not die: yet Jesus said not unto him, this disciple shall not die;

but, if I will that this disciple tarry till I come, what is that to thee?"

Longinus hurried to see who had scribed these words but there was no name on the scroll.

"Mary," he said under his breath. He thought it had to be Mary for it was in her urn with her other writings, and she gave it to him. His mind raced back to what Mary said about the writings.

"You must study them with the Holy Spirit guiding you, so that you receive the true message within them. Many will twist the words, just as they have the words of the prophets."

"If not her, who?" He questioned out loud.

"Stop it!" He scolded himself as he rolled up the parchment. "You always do such things. It gets you no where."

He returned the parchment to his haversack and grabbed his bedding. "You're too tired to make sense," he mumbled as he arranged his bedding on the ground.

He lay down obsessed with his thoughts until he finally fell asleep.

In the morning, the first thing he did was think about the parchment. He kept shaking his head in frustration while he pulled up camp. "Mary can tell me," he muttered as he saddled his horse. "Stop it! She would scold me to go back for such a question."

Longinus mounted his horse and turned toward Cappadocia, then he turned his horse around toward the mountain of Marseille. Then back around again toward Cappadocia.

He stopped and reasoned, "I am but two days ride from Mary. I must return and have her answer this thing."

He turned his horse and rode fast toward the South of Gaul. He had to speak to Mary.

After driving his horse, nonstop, forward in a mad dash filled with obsession, Longinus was getting faint. He had not taken time to eat nor drink adequately. Both he and his horse were waning and wanting of rest, food, and water. He finally reached the point where he could physically go no further and stopped.

Shaking from exhaustion, he dismounted with his spear clenched in his hand. His vision was doubled as he staggered to the back of his horse. As he reached for his haversack, he felt his legs buckle beneath him, and fell to the ground.

He tried to get up but was too weak. He looked over and watched as his horse pitifully dropped down, and rolled over on his side depleted of its last ounce of energy. The two laid parallel on the ground. His spear was still clutched in his hand but his mind was finally quiet. He was totally alone, with no thoughts. His horse gave a few thrusts through his nose and then fell silent as well.

Longinus could no longer think. The world around him was deafened as though he were in a trance.

He started to pass out but was awakened by a deep voice that pierced his heart.

"Longinus, why are you running so?"

Longinus looked up. He did not see anyone. He laid his head back down in the dirt.

"You are very weary, yet you do not seek me to help you," the voice bellowed piercing his very soul.

"Who are you?" shouted Longinus, with his head in the dirt.

"I am the one whose side you pierced."

"Have mercy on me and help me, my Lord," he cried out as he laid there weak, unable to lift himself up.

"How can I help you, when you do not seek me, nor listen to those I have sent before you?"

"I have done this, yes, I have," admitted Longinus. The voice came no more. Longinus waited to hear it again, but it did not come. He passed out from exhaustion.

He dreamed, and in the dream, he saw Mary; she was radiant and looked the way she did in her youth. She called to Longinus, "Come, follow the way of the Lord." He followed her a little ways trying to catch up with her, and then she disappeared.

When Longinus awoke he remembered the voice. He wondered if it was a dream or real. Longinus felt weak, confused, alone, and broken. He dropped to his knees in despair and cried out his disdain for the evil being done to the Followers of the Way and how it broke his heart and wailed of how he could not understand even what was written, all seemed to be in vain.

The Lord took pity on Longinus.

Suddenly a deep voice bellowed out,

"Longinus, get up. I have heard your cry. Go on to where your heart longs. I will be with you."

Longinus stood up and his body and mind were strengthened. His horse now refreshed, was waiting in a manner so majestic.

"Longinus, call my name, and I will come to you. Go now."

He mounted and the horse burst forth running over rocks and debris that should have slowed him down, but he rode like the wind and his horse's hooves barely touched the ground.

The next day, Longinus rounded the bend to Mary's home at the mountain of Marseille by Villalata and saw the clearing. His heart leaped as he continued to gallop to the end of the grove.

As he approached he saw a crowd of people gathered. Longinus dismounted his horse. Holding his spear, he marched past the crowd and up the long path to the cave that Mary called her home. There were so many there. No one was happy; they were weeping and mourning.

He went inside. A woman looked at Longinus and sadly asked, "Did you know her?"

Longinus did not know how to answer. He walked on and into the place where the people were gathered.

He made his way past them and saw that Mary was prepared for burial. Longinus was torn apart. He dropped his spear and threw himself over her body and wept. The people backed away and no one came near him. He let out a haunting wail and continued weeping bitterly over Mary's lifeless body.

Time passed, and people came and went saying their goodbyes, all the while Longinus would not leave her side. No one could say how long this went on, but to Longinus, time had stood still.

A man came to Longinus and said, "It is time to take her to the sepulcher." Longinus would not leave. He clung to Mary. The man put his hand on Longinus's shoulder and said, "Come, we must bury her now."

Longinus looked up with his eyes blurred from the tears. He could not see who was speaking to him, for he was in deep sorrow. Little did he know that the man who placed his hand on his shoulder was Jesus, his Lord.

Several men carefully took her body and lifted it into a wooden box, lined with the finest silk cloth of purple. The women then placed several objects of hers inside of it.

They began to close the lid, and Longinus shouted, "Wait!" They all looked at him, and he said, "Give me one moment with her alone, I beg you."

The people nodded and left the room. Longinus looked down at his sweet Mary lying so still and spoke, "I broke my spear once in anger, and now I break it in search of mercy. I'm not worthy of its power, I don't even know how to wield it other than in the way of a soldier." He took his spear between his hands and broke the head away from the shaft.

"This belongs with one pure of heart and sound in faith, one who was chosen for a special purpose." Longinus carefully placed it next to her heart and covered it with her robe. "I do never understand the writings, but I do know you will be in the hearts of many until the Lord returns. I will be but a ghost."

At that moment, some men came in and one said, "We must take her now," and closed the lid to the wooden box. Longinus stood up and followed the men out. The people were all gathered outside and Longinus followed them to her burial site. It was a day full of sadness for him as well as the masses.

He pitifully wept throughout the entire burial, unashamed of his tears. He was emotionally drained as his heart was ripped and torn apart from the inside out. His mighty stature of 6'4 and solid muscle was now weakened and pale from grief.

When he left, he rode a small ways and stopped and fell prostrate upon the ground. For the very first time Longinus begged from deep within his heart for forgiveness of his past selfishness and to be forgiven for all he had fallen short of. He asked for a sign of reassurance that his giving the tip of the spear of his destiny to Mary was what he was truly led to do and not an act of his own impulsive thinking.

When he arose from his deep prayer, he felt a sense of calmness and assurance. Whether he was led to do as he did, or forgiven for his impulsiveness, either way, what had been done was done. Now, he would head back to Cappadocia and serve the

Lord as a man and not as an enigma of Rome who did not age and could not be killed.

His curse was finally over. Or so, that is what he believed.

A TRAP SET IN ROME

Grieving beyond anything that Longinus had ever felt, even more than from the loss of his first and most cherished love, Sabena, he ventured toward Cappadocia. It seemed as though he were dead and marching back toward a place of burial. Perhaps this was because his heart was broken, or perhaps because he no longer wielded the spear?

Regardless, his vigor for life was stripped from him, and he no longer cared how much time it took to go here or there anymore. All of his questions seemed to have died with Mary; except for one; why did she who was obedient to the Father and pure of heart die and he who was rough, stubborn and wayward live?

When Longinus stopped for water and food, he would think of the reality of Mary's death even deeper and harder. Haunted by his memories and weary of the long journey home by horse, he decided to go through Rome and to the ports. From there, he would board a ship, he thought and sail to Cappadocia and get there much faster.

Finally he reached Rome and his spirit lifted slightly as he looked forward to reaching the ports. As he rode through the outskirts, his mind wandered back to his past days as a Centurion and remembered why Rome was such a deep well of trouble. His allegiance was gone even before they stripped him of his Centurion rank. It was by Rome's iron hand that he was molded into a stoic killing machine and by their betrayal that he became their fierce enemy. For one cannot hunt a rabbit that was raised in their cage and then suddenly say it is wild, or so he thought as he road along. The hypocrisy and insanity of the dictatorship of Rome was to Longinus as a bitter sore that would not heal.

It was only a little while and he came upon soldiers blocking the road and redirecting all travelers toward the Augusta Archway. He went as he was told, unaware that this was a baited trap, by order of Nero, to capture followers. As he rode through the archway he heard a woman crying out.

He looked and saw two Roman soldiers bullying her. They threw her back and forth between them, like a bag of wheat. "You can have her, no, you can have her," they taunted. "Pray to Nero to have mercy on you."

The soldier laughed as he slapped her down to the ground. "Come on, let us hear your prayer to Nero," sneered the other soldier as he kicked her hard in the side. The woman screamed in pain.

Longinus jumped down from his horse and ran to the soldiers and pummeled them mercilessly. They fell to the ground.

He helped the woman up and said to her, "Go, run from here." He turned to get his horse, and Roman soldiers were holding it.

Next to them stood a skinny man, in a white tunic with no belt, no shoes, with a scarf around his fat neck, and a civic crown upon his head. It was Nero.

"Thou shalt have no strange gods beside me," sneered Nero. "Now bow to me and kiss my feet."

Longinus reached for his sword and immediately he was surrounded with Roman Hasta's one inch from his body in every direction.

Nero smiled and sneered in his bratty and irritating tone, "Shall I have them lance you like a boil? Or something else? Now kiss my feet!"

Longinus stood still and remembered Mary's words:

"Longinus, it takes great strength and courage to stand for the kingdom of heaven, knowing you will be tortured and then slain for taking that stand. The sheep you call dry bones are standing! Open your eyes and see it!"

Longinus looked at Nero's feet and said, "How can I with all these hastas in my way?"

"Guards, take his sword belt, then oblige him to come forth so he can kiss my feet," ordered Nero.

A Praetorian Guard removed Longinus's sword belt, then frisked him. Finding no other weapon on him, he ordered the hastas to be lowered, and allowed him to go to Nero.

Longinus moved toward him and looked down at Nero's feet. He then looked up at Nero's face and deep into his eyes. Nero had all the whites showing and a look of hysteria in his face. Longinus then bent down on one knee, and spat on Nero's feet.

Nero was livid and shouted hysterically, "Crucify him now!"

The soldiers secured Longinus and began to drag him toward the execution area. They drug him past his horse and he saw a legionnaire digging through his haversack at the parchments then threw it to the ground like discarded waste. The legionnaire ordered his horse to be taken to the stables and a soldier promptly led the horse away.

Longinus struggled to get free, and another soldier ran over and pummeled him violently with a club. A centurion ordered the soldier to stop.

"Enough! He is to be crucified, not beaten to death in the streets,"

The soldiers dragged Longinus along to the execution area.

Nero shouted to the guard washing the spit off his feet, "Hurry up, I don't want to miss a thing!"

The soldiers forced Longinus to the ground and placed him over a beam. One soldier held his hand in place, while two others struggled to hold his body fast to the ground.

Nero approached and watched, smiling like a mad man.

A tall man in a dark hooded robe walked over to Longinus's haversack. He opened it and saw the parchments and scrolls. He quickly closed it and picked it up. He walked toward the place where Longinus was being nailed to a beam on the ground. He stood a small distance away and watched. A large dog that looked like a lion came up and stood beside the hooded man.

Longinus looked up to the heavens and shouted, "If this is the destiny I have chosen, then let me fulfill it with courage!"

A soldier held a nail in place over Longinus's wrist while another soldier lifted a hammer and brought it down with great force, pounding the top of the nail. The shrill clang from the hammer clashing against the iron nail riveted in Longinus's ears. He let out a painful scream and looked up to the heavens. He mustered all of his strength and shouted as loud as he could, so Nero would hear.

"Lord, receive my soul!"

Nero's smile of glee quickly changed to a look of disgust and distain. He ran over to Longinus and spat on him.

"Shut up!" he shouted as he grabbed the hammer from the soldier's hand and raised it to pound the nail in deeper.

Nero thrust the hammer down, but not having the strength to control its weight, he lost his balance and toppled over on top of Longinus, totally missing the nail.

Nero shouted, as he clumsily climbed to his feet, "Guard finish this now!"

His Praetorian Guard picked up the hammer, and raised it high to pound the nail, at the same time the man in the hooded robe raised his hand. Suddenly, the soldier fell forward with a dagger in his back, feebly dropping the hammer and gasping as he crashed face down in the dirt.

Instantly, daggers whizzed through the air targeting the Roman soldiers, while simultaneously arrows filled the sky like a black cloud coming from over the top of the Augusta Archway. The sound was like a thunderous wind as they rained down on all the soldiers at once striking them with precision.

In the flash of an eye, the streets were filled with fallen, bleeding Roman soldiers pierced with arrows and daggers in their backs and chests, including all of Nero's Praetorian Guard.

Nero was terrified at the sight of his best soldiers dropping dead before his eyes and shrieked.

"Guards, guards!" Nero looked around, panicked, only to see that none of his Praetorian Guards were left standing. Every one of them lay in a pool of blood.

He shrieked again, this time long and loud like a woman in terror and turned to run. A dagger whizzed through the air barely missing his temple, and sliced off a lock of his hair. Nero flailed his arms frantically, screaming for guards to help him as he ran away.

Meanwhile, the man in the hooded robe ran over to Longinus.

Longinus looked and saw it was Khalid.

Khalid shoved a rag in Longinus's mouth.

"Bite Down!" He instructed.

Longinus bit down on the rag, as Khalid pried the nail from his wrist.

Longinus winced at the pain of the nail being pulled out ripping his skin. Khalid tied a cloth around it quickly then helped Longinus up.

Another hooded man leading two saddled horses, rode up at a steady clip. Khalid and Longinus mounted quickly and rode out of Rome with great speed.

Then, from out of nowhere, a band of bounty hunters on horses appeared from all sides of the city riding out like a storm behind them with several wagons full of Followers of the Way. It was Longinus's band of men. The galloping hooves of the rider's horses and rolling wagons left a haze of dust so thick, the sun could not be seen. An ominous darkness filled the air and drifted over the dead soldiers bodies like a black plague.

NERO'S TEMPER TANTRUM

The splendor of the palace of Nero was now overshadowed by the dreadful site of its' chamber floors filled with shattered ivory, chunks of marble, and the torn fabric of shredded tapestry and drapes. Large broken urns and vases littered the floor with clumps of scattered dirt and mangled floral arrangements covering the broken head of Diana. A few feet away her headless stone body stood with missing arms and chunks of its torso chipped out. A stream of ruby red wine flowed downward from its' cracked neck, leaving deep stained streaks that lent to the illusion that she had been mercilessly battered and decapitated.

Now, in the aftermath of Nero's long procession of palace destruction, he was exhausted but still fuming inside. Huffing and puffing, he was seated on his ornately jeweled, golden throne with his laurel leaf crown sitting cockeyed on his head and the wild eyed appearance of a shaken man gone mad.

Standing at attention, surrounding Nero's throne are what was left of his best military advisors who appeared to be as shaken and nervous as he. Whether this was due to the surprise attack and death of royal guards or due to Nero's deranged temper tantrum of destruction, or due to both, the military advisors knew they were not gathered because Nero wanted their advice. They knew there was another blistering round of battering to come, and if past equals future, they foresaw their present situation was quite dire.

Nero shouted in a hoarse voice, as he awkwardly flailed a hammer in the air, "All of you – every one of you should be killed for allowing this to happen!"

Nero jumped to his feet and threw a silver cup filled with wine at a centurion and missed. Instead, the wine filled cup hit a pile of broken rubble. The wine slowly drizzled downward, slithering like a snake until it reached the heel of the centurion's foot and pooled around and over his sandal. It tickled annoyingly at his skin, but the centurion did not move.

"Look at this mess! It's your fault! And yours, and yours, and yours and yours and yours!" He shouted as he pointed his boney finger at each one.

"Your incompetence made me to this," he looked around and dramatically mourned over the loss of his Diana.

Unexpectedly something caught his eye, he dashed from his throne and ran over to a pile of rubble and picked up a torn rose. He smelled it and smiled, then looked over at Diana's broken off hand and gently placed it between her missing forefinger and thumb.

"It's not my fault, really Diana," he said soothingly to the broken off hand, "They made me do it," he turned and addressed his military advisors, "I demand you slay each other in front of Diana right now!"

The chief military advisor calmly spoke, "Prefect, Sir, if we slay each other, who will lead your cohorts to avenge this tragedy?"

Nero touched the side of his head and felt the empty patch where his lock of hair was clipped by a whizzing dagger. He screamed out!

"You and all of you allowed a golden lock to be cut from your god! I can't trust any of you!"

The military advisors showed no outward emotion and continued to stand at attention, but inwardly they were melting apart like ice on the fire.

A sentry entered the chamber and observed the disarray, then stopped short. It was quite a few feet less from Nero than he generally stood.

"Prefect, the legate has arrived," he firmly announced.

Nero dusted off his tunic and fluffed his hair as he hurried to his throne. He tried positioning his posture several ways in an effort to look important and more Caesar god like, before he finally settled on a pose.

"Send him in."

The sentry bowed and left.

Within seconds the Legate entered. He glanced out of the corner of his left eye, then his right eye at the disarray. Keeping his head straight and refraining from making any facial or bodily expression that would acknowledge the mess, he marched midway to the throne and stopped. He bowed to Nero. Nero nodded.

The Legate spoke in a firm voice, "Prefect, Sir. The man that spat on your feet was the one they call the enigma."

Nero's eyes widened, "The one they say cannot age, and possesses great power from his spear?"

"He is the same," answered the Legate.

Nero stood up from his throne.

"But, he had no spear. You bring me lies! Guard kill this liar now!"

Desperately the Legate pleaded, "Prefect, Sir. It is no lie. The daggers and arrows that killed the soldiers were the work of his skilled band of men. Most of them are bounty hunters!"

Nero paced the floor as he contemplated what he was just told. The guards and Legate were silent. They nervously held their breath waiting to see how Nero would respond.

"You mean, I had him in my hands and he escaped me? Yet he can bleed… I saw it with my own eyes."

"Indeed he did, Prefect, Sir."

"So… he is not an enigma!" shouted Nero gleefully. "He must be killed."

The Legate nodded. "I have devised a military strategy to do so, Prefect, Sir."

"Splendid!" exclaimed Nero as he clapped his hands rapidly, "Tell me what is this plan! I want to hear all of it."

"We will-"

"Stop. I'm not ready yet," Nero scurried to his throne, seated himself, and squirmed about to get comfortable. He clasped his hands tightly around the golden arm rests of his throne and leaned forward.

"Come closer and tell me every detail. I want every detail!"

The Legate moved closer to the throne and started to speak of the plan, "We will-"

"Stop," Nero interrupted, "Closer, come closer."

The Legate moved closer and started to speak.

"We-"

Nero interrupted again and motioned for him to come even closer. The Legate moved closer and Nero continued to motion with his hand to come until they were face to face.

"Now speak, do tell me everything," Nero urged, "Everything!"

The soldier began to speak, "We will…"

DESTINY IS A STRANGE THING

Tucked away in the foothills of the Apennines mountain range, Longinus and the band of men had made a camp and were eating foodstuffs of dried jerky, onions and sprouted grain bread. They were not lighting a camp fire this night as they knew Roman legions would be out hunting for them.

Longinus looked at his wrapped hand as he took a bite of bread. Khalid offered him a cup of water.

He took the cup with his wrapped wrist.

"Careful there," warned Khalid, "The closure I put on it takes time to heal."

"You worry like a woman," Snapped Longinus, "I-" he suddenly stopped talking and choked up.

"Easy there. Why you doing that? Somethings eating away there and it's not me."

"Khalid… it's Mary."

"What's she gone and done?"

"She hasn't done anything…she's gone."

"Gone? Where's she gone too?"

Longinus closed his eyes tight and clenched his teeth.

Khalid turned to his dog, Vitali and spoke, "He's got some bad news girl. I feel it."

Vitali nodded.

Khalid held out a piece of dried jerky to Longinus,

"Eat, we talk later."

"Mary died."

"Khalid's eyes welled up in tears. "I knew it was bad." He tried to hold them back, but couldn't. Tears streamed down his bulky chiseled cheeks. Instantly Khalid was weakened and sobbed like a woman. Vitali whined, and whimpered.

"Can't fix it and it hurts cause I can't," moaned Khalid.

Longinus let his tears flow but continued to speak.

"I was with her and we had food and spoke of many things. Of Nero and the followers he tortured and killed in the Circus.

She scolded me for not having faith and always coming to her…I told her she was the only one I could ask such deep questions," He paused a moment and sighed, "She said, go to him. The Lord," He paused, "I told her, but I can't see him. She said he can see me, and that is good enough."

Khalid put his arm around Longinus and drew him tight to his side, "If Mary said that is good enough, it is good enough."

"I read the writing from her parchment and I had questions. They will never be answered now."

"They will be answered. Just not by Mary," encouraged Khalid.

"I had to see her again. I rode so hard I dropped from exhaustion, so did my horse. I wrestled with a voice that told me to go on, he would be with me. I heard a strong voice."

"So you heard him but could not see him?"

"Yes."

"Next you will see him."

"I rode to Mary. When I got there she lay dead in a wooden burial box."

Khalid wiping his face, "I will always remember her smile and kindness to people."

"It was the hardest thing to believe. I kept thinking I was still passed out exhausted and dreaming. I kept hoping I would wake up and none of this was happening."

"I felt that before. The day Vitali died. I tried to wake up, but I was up. In sadness I fell to sleep." Khalid paused and wiped his tears with the back of his sleeve.

"When I woke up, Mary was there. First time I ever saw her. She told me my dog was sleeping. So I dug out from the dirt in her grave and she was alive."

Longinus answered, "Mary had gifts."

"I thought many times she brought Vitali back to me. My heart knew it."

Longinus in a regretful tone, "But she could not save herself. Or was it her time to return to heaven. Like she said of Jesus? I just don't know these things."

In his moment of self- pity, Longinus continued to moan, "Who will answer these things for me?"

"Maybe she will talk to you like Jesus did?" offered Khalid hopefully.

"I don't know. She has the promises of heaven. This I know, she is there now. She has no time for this stubborn man."

"Stubborn man or foolish? Why were you going through Rome? Were you ready to die?"

"I was not. Or so I believe I was not."

Longinus fidgeted with the cloth on his wounded wrist.

"When I entered Rome I was in deep sorrow and not thinking of Roman traps."

"Destiny is a strange thing," added Khalid, " Were we not in Rome lying wait to stop Nero's soldiers from nailing followers to beams, you'd be dead too."

"Indeed. My time has not yet come. There is more for me to do."

"Where is your spear? Did the Romans take it?"

"The spear is now with another."

"Who?"

Longinus hesitated, and then answered, "Another who was chosen."

"Did you break up your spear and throw it away wishing to die?"

"No. I told you I gave it to another who was chosen."

Khalid stared at Longinus deep in his eyes, "I believe you." Khalid asked no more of the spear. He loosed his grip on Longinus and gave him a pat on the back.

Longinus took a drink of water and looked at Khalid, "Nero will be after us with vengeance."

Khalid answered, "We will need more men to fight. I will go and find us some."

Khalid put the last of his meat into his mouth and motioned for his dog, Vitali, to follow him. He mounted his horse. Longinus looked surprised.

"You are going now?"

"There is no time to waste. You return to Cappadocia. Let your hand heal. Me and Vitali go and find more men, then we return."

Longinus nodded and stood up, "I owe you my life."

Khalid blushed, "Awe- nough of that. We go while the night is young. Vitali come."

Vitali stretched her front legs down as though she were preparing for a long run. She shook her massive body and sprinted over to Khalid.

Longinus wondered at her beauty. Such big thick paws like a bear and strong legs to match. Her long flowing mane was that of a lion. He thought how lucky Khalid was to have such a magnificent animal of protection. "She's like the lion of Judah," he said softly under his breath.

He stood and watched Khalid and Vitali head off into the night, watching until they were out of sight.

ROMANS APPROACHING

Some time had passed and Khalid was still out looking for men to fight with Longinus. Meanwhile, a Roman cohort of 800 men had just entered the outskirts of Cappadocia. They were being led by a lean bounty hunter named Armond and his big black hunting dog. The dog's coat was unkempt and full of dreg locks. He had a cloth sopped with the dried blood of Longinus tied to his collar. The Roman cohort was following the dogs lead under the command of the bounty hunter. They were in search of Longinus and his band of men using the Legate's plan. However, the Senior Centurion had many reservations regarding its' so called brilliance.

The Senior Centurion had just signaled for the men to stop and rest their horses. Feeling concerned about his soldiers being led out in the open so close to Armenia he dismounted and approached the bounty hunter.

"Your dog leads us into Parthian scouted land," stated the Senior Centurion boldly.

Armond quipped back, "He leads us to the man you seek."

"We are still at war with King Vologeses. When his scouts send word that we travel with such a great cohort through Cappadocia, they will believe we are headed to Armenia. He may come and attack us."

Armond looked as though he could care less and answered, "Cappadocia is a Roman Province. Your fear is unfounded."

The Senior Centurion motioned for the men to remount their horses and they proceeded.

Meanwhile, back in the village of Cappadocia...

Longinus and his band of men had just returned to their village. He dismounted his horse and a disciple named Priscilla who was sent from the mission in the south of Gaul, saw him from the church yard. She eagerly ran to greet him.

"Mary, how is she?"

Longinus sadly answered her, "I am sorry Priscilla," he choked up then paused a moment to pull himself together.

He spoke to her calmly, "Mary has died. She was laid to rest in Villalata."

Priscilla looked down. Her countenance fell. She turned and slowly walked back to the church in a daze. Longinus watched until she went inside.

Feeling helpless and wanting to fix her pain he ran to the entry way of the church then stopped. He hesitated on whether or not he should bother her inside the church.

He looked inside and saw Priscilla on her knees in prayer. Again he started to enter then stopped. He helplessly watched her and could not bear it.

Longinus turned around and left. He walked over to a stone fence about three feet high that surrounded a garden. He straddled the fence with one leg in the garden and one leg outside of it. He gazed down then impulsively banged his fist on the cold stone. He pounded at it until his fists were sore, then abruptly swung his legs around facing the garden. He stared out stupefied as his mind wandered remembering many things about Mary and his life with her.

He looked up to the heavens and pleaded softly, "Why has Mary, the most elect one died? And I the one who speared you still live?"

His voice grew louder, "What purpose was your death if evil still triumphs and the good still die?"

A disciple named Philip unintentionally overheard Longinus. He walked over and sat next to him on the stone fence.

"When the master was here, he spoke of these days."

Longinus curiously looked at Philip and questioned, "These days?"

"He said the world would hate us for it hated him. Persecutions would follow us."

"Did he say why this would be?"

"He said because the ruler of this world opposes his Father's Kingdom and because he had chosen us out of the world, the world would hate us." Philip paused.

Longinus mumbled, "Why would he teach such things? Knowing we would be hated for it. It makes no sense. I can't understand these teachings."

Philip answered, "He told us all, that he did not come to bring peace, but a sword."

"I was told by Mary that he came to bring peace and evil cannot be killed with a sword. You don't say what Mary said."

"What Mary said is also true," answered Philip.

"This is why all I hear I do not understand. Nothing makes sense. It is all a riddle of words."

Philip put his hand on Longinus's shoulder. "It is the world that is confusing we can never fight the entire world. We are in it but not of it. We must do as he did and ask the Father to intervene for us and to guide us."

Impatiently Longinus swung his body around and leaped off the stone fence. He stood outside the garden and looked at Philip with disgust.

"I try to make sense of his words, always. And always I am confused. It makes no sense to me."

Longinus stormed off very abrupt. Philip watched as he left. When Longinus was out of sight, Philip bowed his head and prayed.

"I do not know how to teach him."

Back in the outskirts of Cappadocia…

The Senior Centurion and his cohort of men had continued to follow the lead of the Bounty Hunter, Armond, and his massive dog. The men were weary from the heat and the Senior Centurion had grown more uneasy due to marching deeper into Armenian scouted territory.

Suddenly, without any warning, the ominous sound of whizzing arrows was heard. The soldiers looked and a cloud of arrows were blackening the sky flying through the air toward them.

The Senior Centurion shouted, "Shields!"

The soldiers huddled their horses together and covered their heads with their shields. Arrows bombarded them, some bounced off, while others stuck in the shields, and the majority of them pierced the bodies of soldiers and their horses.

A battle cry rang out from over the horizon and a stampede of Parthian horsemen rode over the hill to attack. The sun was at the backs of the cohort and reflected off of the ornate armor of the Parthians and the equally decorated armor of their horses. The shining light blinded the soldiers and their eyes could not look out upon the Parthians for it.

As the Parthians got closer they dropped the reigns of their horses and used both arms to draw their bows. Seated firmly, staying steady in their saddles they relentlessly shot myriads of arrows at the soldiers with pinpoint accuracy.

It was the most amazing battle sight to behold. The blinding beam of light filling the entire horizon as it bounced like a laser off the Parthians high polished armor. Fearless horse and rider gliding along as one magnificent unit over the rocky terrain, with the Parthians hands free to fire arrow after arrow after arrow and never miss a stride.

Within minutes half of the cohort was slain and the other half was met with swords beheading Roman soldiers and savagely slashing the bellies of their horses.

The senior Centurion sounded to retreat. The Roman soldiers turned to flee in the direction of Rome, only to be pierced from behind. What the arrows missed the blades of the Parthians finished off, sending helmeted Roman heads flying through the air.

Meanwhile, the bounty hunter and his dog deserted the soldiers as quickly as the Parthians appeared on the horizon. He rode swiftly, headed toward the top of the hill passing the Parthians as they rode in to attack.

The Parthians did not stop the bounty hunter, nor did they shoot any arrow at him. He was strangely not dealt with as he continued over the horizon and onward through Cappadocia unscathed.

The Parthians pursued only the Romans.

PARTHIAN CONFLICT

It was early in the morning and Longinus was outside in the village tending to a disheveled group of Followers of the Way who had come seeking refuge. He heard horses approaching and quickly looked toward the direction of the sounding hooves. He eyed Khalid leading a band of new men and made a sigh of relief. Longinus walked toward them and watched as they rode in.

"Parthians, the best!" shouted Khalid.

Longinus nodded cautiously at the Parthians, "I see."

Khalid and the Parthians dismounted, "That way," ordered Khalid as he pointed, "The stables are there." He looked at Longinus, "Much to say. Your hand is it better?"

Longinus ignored the question. He was angry to see the Parthians. "Why do you bring Parthian enemies to our village?"

Khalid answered firmly, "Not all Parthians are enemies."

Longinus quipped angrily back, "They beheaded my wife!"

"And so did Parthians do the same to my mother! But these men did no harm to you or me."

Longinus would have no part of it, "All Parthians are savage beasts!"

Khalid was not giving up, "Longinus you must let that go. We all suffered. They too had their families slain and villages burned."

"Let that go?" shouted Longinus, "Shall we lay down our necks and let go the Romans and Nero as well?" He angrily stomped away.

Khalid looked down at Vitali, "He struggles with more than his destiny."

Phillip, who was standing by a tree, overheard the entire conversation. He was disappointed and sadly lowered his head. He mumbled under his breath, "How can this one be taught?"

As Longinus angrily stomped toward his house he eyed Priscilla with a basket of bread. She was giving some to Parthians. His anger kindled stronger when he saw this.

Priscilla happily approached Longinus.

"You must nourish your body. Here," she said and held out a loaf.

"Save it!" he snapped. "You may find more dogs to feed!"

Priscilla was surprised by his rudeness, but sensed what he meant for she had fed the Parthians. However, she wasn't going to accept a brow beating for acts of kindness without having her own say.

"I know your heart still aches for Mary, as does mine. You must not let that make you grow hard toward others."

"My heart and how it breaks for Mary has nothing to do with my anger for Parthian scoundrels."

"If Mary were here and saw your actions she would tell you to forgive those who have wronged you. The same as our Master taught us to do."

"It is easy for you to forgive when you have not had a loved one slain by evil men."

Priscilla's patience now grew thin. Frustrated she raised her voice and lashed back, "Longinus, you were forgiven by my loved one killed on the cross by evil men. You who pierced his side. Your words are selfish and cruel. You know not what you do, nor what you say!"

Longinus was at a loss for words and thought hard how to defend himself against what Priscilla said. He watched as a tear fell down her soft cheek. She quickly wiped it away.

Longinus spoke softly, "I did not think of-"

Priscilla interrupted him, "No. you did not think! Your words are unbridled. You say and do according to your own thoughts. Your own reason."

"I speak the truth of what I see," He said in defense.

"You are as a blind man groping in the dark grabbing at what you feel for you cannot see. You seek only what you want and what will please you now, always!"

"Parthians are dangerous thieves and murderers, even the blind sees that! I fight for the Followers of the Way. "

"You fight for yourself. Whatever will make YOU feel right. Not others. Who can help a man who refuses to listen with his heart?"

"My heart breaks. I fought for Mary always and it is broken without her."

"That is the problem. You selfishly fought for Mary so you could hear her tell you - 'well done'."

"I, I…" Longinus was at a loss for words.

Priscilla realized her tongue had become as unbridled as Longinus and felt bad because of it.

"Forgive me for my cruel words. I have spoken wrongly."

Longinus did not know what to say against her apology. He was silent.

"I must go. There are more dogs to feed," Priscilla turned and left.

Longinus stood quietly alone, feeling bad about their exchange of words. Priscilla sounded so much like Mary, he thought. He felt a strong urge to run after her, but he controlled it.

His mind raced as he processed Priscilla's words. Longinus remembered Mary at the cross and how when he speared the Lord she forgave him. Suddenly he found his mind entering into some form of a hypnotic trance.

Whether out of the body or in, he did not know.

In a flash, Longinus was being pulled with great speed down a long winding tunnel and when he reached the end of it, his body slowed down almost to a halt.

He floated out of the tunnel while hovering above the ground on his back in the air. He moved his body forward and placed his feet on the ground. He looked around and found himself, once again at the cross on the day of the execution of the Nazarene. Or so he thought until he looked and saw an apparition of himself following orders to kill the innocent Nazarene as though it were nothing.

He watched himself follow through with his duty to execute the Nazarene on top of Golgotha. Mary and the two other women were at the foot of the Nazarene's cross.

Longinus floated toward them for his body was light as air. He saw people, but was not sure if they saw him; for no one acted like he was there.

He heard the powerful delivery of the Nazarene's words, "Father forgive them for they know no what they do." Looking up he saw the sign above the Nazarene's head and read the words, "This is the King of The Jews."

He looked over and watched the apparition of himself look up and read the sign. It was at that moment as he watched in awe, that he realized he was the one who was the apparition that no one could see and not the Longinus he was watching. Or so he believed.

He looked around and Mary and the others had vanished. He watched the man on the cross as he slowly faded from his sight, until he could no longer see him.

He rubbed his eyes and found his scar had returned and his vision was cloudy. His eye was blind again and it ached with the same pain as before he was healed.

Longinus shook his head to end the trance and finally awakened out from it.

Feeling weak inside and frustrated, he grabbed at his eye and felt it all over. He was relieved to find the scar was still gone, and he could see clearly from it. He looked up to the sky.

"Lord, I thank you for the healing of my eye. But, I am a man of flesh, not the King of The Jews. I cannot do as you did? I cannot."

NERO'S BLOODY SHAME

The Senior Centurion had shamefully returned to Rome brutally defeated with only 248 soldiers remaining alive out of a cohort of 800 and most all who returned were wounded. He was now in the palace of Nero, standing before him weakly trying to defend his position for such a humiliating loss.

He was pale, mincing his words, taking gulps of breath between each pitiful fact he must report. It did not bode well for him for he could not explain it with any satisfaction to Nero, but he had boldly tried and was almost finished with his account.

"...and at that, I regret to say, the only thing we could do was retreat," said the Senior Centurion.

Nero asked, "And what of my bounty hunter?"

"The bounty hunter was either slain by the Parthians as well, or he deserted us. There is no way to know for certain."

"How many Parthians did you kill?" asked Nero.

The Senior Centurion answered, "A good number of them."

Nero, not amused, leaned forward on his throne, "A good number would be all of them!"

He angrily shot up from his throne and stormed over to the Senior Centurion.

"A good report would be that *they* fled and not Rome."

"But Prefect…"

Nero interrupted, "You failed at bringing me the Enigma. But succeeded in giving Vologeses almost all of my cohort to slay!" Nero stomped his little leg as hard as he could.

The Senior Centurion started to sweat profusely. He knew what was coming next. He trembled as Nero leaned into his face to toy with him.

"As the god of Rome, I will either give you a thumb up to live or a thumb down to die. What oh what shall I give you?"

A military advisor sensed the writing on the wall and wanted to avoid a domino effect of high ranking military executions, mainly his own. He believed if he could somehow postpone the inevitable slaying of the Senior Centurion, Nero might not go on another one of his bloody tirades of stabbing and chopping up everyone and everything in sight. The joy of killing and the sight of blood always made Nero thirsty for more. He had an insatiable appetite for initiating such horrors.

The military advisor quickly spoke up with an idea.

"Might I suggest oh great God of Rome, that you use him in the Circus and let him entertain you with a most creative and horrendous death there? Perhaps fighting a lion or several raging elephants? Doing something here and now is too simple, to dull."

Nero's eyes glazed over and widened, "Now that is a splendid idea!" He made an ugly face at the Senior Centurion, and then turned to the guards.

"Take him to the prison and let him wonder what manner of torture and death he shall entertain me by."

Two guards removed the Senior Centurion from the Palace.

Nero turned and stared at the advisor, "There must be a way to lure the enigma back to Rome …perhaps we set a trap?"

"Indeed, Prefect," answered the Advisor.

"Think of something very clever. I want to show all of Rome how this man can bleed."

The advisor nodded and smiled, more from his self-perceived cleverness than from Nero granting permission. But then, as always, you just have to wait to the end of your discussion with Nero before you ever dare to gloat.

Nero added quickly, "You have until sundown to report to me this plan."

The Advisor had no such grand plan, nor any idea of what that plan would be and made an attempt to stall.

"Prefect, Sir, sundown is not enough time to make the grandest plan fit to please such a god as yourself. I ask that it pleases you to grant me a day. "

Nero squinted his eyes and snarled, "What is time? I don't care if the torture is rats or lions. You have until sundown."

Nero walked up to the Advisor and stared deep into his eyes.

"It isn't that hard, unless you are not capable of making such a plan. Are you?"

The advisor's grin disappeared from his face and his skin turned pale. He cleared his throat and responded with fake confidence that could clearly be heard in his voice.

"My great god, I am capable. Sundown will be sufficient."

Nero looked at him with the whites of his eyes showing all around and said, "I knew it would be."

He turned around and pranced to his thrown and positioned himself.

The Military Advisor was still standing at attention. Nero glared at him and shouted, "Go now. For one that wanted more time, you are wasting what you have!"

"Yes Prefect, Sir,"

He bowed and left the Palace.

OF STRANGERS AND FRIENDS

After a hard ride, Armond stopped his horse and took a drink of water from his flask. He peered out into the rocky horizon eyeing the faint outline of fairy chimneys. "It won't be long now," he said under his breath. He continued to ride on.

Some while later, Armond approached the village of Longinus in Cappadocia. He dismounted his horse and took the cloth of dried blood from around his dog's neck. He tucked it inside his shirt then mounted back onto his horse and proceeded to enter the village with his big black dog walking beside him. Once inside he dismounted and took the reign of his horse, leading it behind him through the village. His dog followed.

Armond was in need of a place to stay and provisions. He saw several men busy with taking care of their horses and other mundane tasks. Sizing them up he felt comfortable and walked over to one of the younger men who was busy sorting through his haversack.

"Who leads this village?"

The man looked up from his sorting, and went back to his work while he answered, "A man they call Longinus."

Armond's eyes lit up. "Really? Tell me about him. How can I find favor?"

"He hates Parthians, but he likes bounty hunters. You a bounty hunter?"

"Indeed."

"You should have no problem."

"But, I hail from Parthia. Should I lie if he asks?"

"That's the way to get killed. He hates liars. You're best off talking to Khalid."

"Khalid?"

"He's the big guy with the lion. He's a bounty hunter too."

"Lion?"

"Not sure what it is, but it looks like a lion."

Armond nodded and moved on.

Khalid spied Armond and his big black dog. Vitali growled low. Khalid turned to Vitali, "Easy girl. Let's see about this man and his dog."

"You there… what brings you here?"

"I heard you seek strong and cunning men to protect the Followers of the Way."

Khalid smiled but Vitali growled and showed her teeth at Armond's dog. Khalid motioned for Vitali to calm down.

"You heard right. Do you come to join us?"

Armond asked, "What's the pay?"

"Pay comes from the coins and possessions off the Romans you slay."

"Not a lucrative offer, but it will do," Armond extended his hand and added, "My name is Armond,"

Vitali growled giving Khalid concern but accepted his offer and shook his hand.

Khalid pointed, "Stables are that way," He pointed again, "Food over there. After you eat, others will show you where to bed down."

Armond nodded and proceeded to the stables.

Khalid watched Armond walk toward the stables. He turned to Vitali, "Something tells me to keep a close eye on that one," Vitali barked in agreement.

Khalid motioned Vitali, "Come on. Time to eat."

They walked over to the dining hall.

Longinus was sitting at a table just finishing up his meal. Khalid nodded at him, but wasn't in the mood to argue about Parthians so he didn't speak.

Longinus eyed Priscilla working diligently taking dishes from the tables. He thought to himself, "She is always devoted to others making sure they are fed, clothed and heard. Why do I always say hard words? Mary told me the same as she. I say and do according to my own thoughts. I am a stubborn man."

Longinus's heart was heavy. He wanted to tell her he had been a fool but wrestled with his pride. She was a wise woman with beauty and a smile like Mary, he thought. He tried to remember the day when she first came to Cappadocia; he was ashamed that he could not remember. He grew restless and knew he must tell her that his heart breaks from the hard words he said to her.

He got up and took his plate to the area where Priscilla was gathering the dirty ones. As he approached she quickly went into the kitchen. He had hoped she would stay there to take his plate. Thinking she hid from him in the kitchen he laid his plate down hard.

He turned around and saw Priscilla carrying out more food in a large pot. He was quickly relieved that she was busy and not hiding from him. His heart was heavy and he needed to talk to her about his angry words, but now was not the time.

He watched her put the pot of food on the table and quickly make her way back to the kitchen to get more. She came out with a big tray of hot loaves and placed it on the table. She was on her way back to the kitchen and Longinus slowly stepped out and blocked her way.

He looked down at her and pleaded, "Priscilla, please forgive me."

She answered, "Longinus, I already have. I feel your struggle."

"My struggle gives me no right to banter at others. We all have struggles."

Priscilla reached her hand up and touched his cheek. Longinus felt her gentle touch and remembered the times Mary would touch his cheek. A tear welled up in his eye but he fought it back.

Priscilla acted like she didn't see that. "When I came here from the South of Gaul, I came because Mary told me of the great need to teach and help the followers who were driven from their homes. She warned me that in coming there would be many tribulations but the rewards in heaven would be great."

"I never knew that Mary said this."

"Mary told me that you were a stubborn man but a good one. She told me to help you when you struggle. Show you the way. I do not feel that I helped you very well."

Longinus looked deep at Priscilla and felt as though he was seeing her for the very first time. Her long auburn hair was so much like Mary's and her brown eyes were as innocent and beautiful as a doe. He felt a warmth in his heart for her that was never there before.

"Priscilla, you did help, more than you know."

Priscilla smiled and started to return to her work. Longinus touched her arm. She turned and he held out his big arms gesturing for an embrace. She gave him a big embrace, then smiled big and returned to her work. Longinus smiled and turned around to leave and saw a man with a big black dog standing in the doorway. It was Armond.

"Who are you?" asked Longinus.

"I am Armond."

"What are you doing here?"

"I joined your war party."

"From where do you hail?"

Armond paused a brief moment, then answered, "Armenia."

Longinus smiled, "So we are neighbors. Welcome."

Armond nodded and moved forward looking for a seat. He sat down and watched Longinus out of the corner of his eye until he left the Dining Hall.

He sneered and whispered under his breath, "So that's the Enigma."

NERO'S EVIL PLAN

Back at the Palace the sun was going down and Nero was anxious to hear from the military advisor. He stood on the porch looking out at the sun setting in the west.

"Where is he? He should be here by now," He said out loud to himself.

He no sooner spoke and a sentry came in. "Prefect, Sir. Your Military Advisor has arrived."

"Splendid, splendid!" Nero shrieked while rapidly clapping his hands.

Nero hurried into his Palace chamber and sat on his throne. He went through his usual positioning to get comfortable and show his best god-self presence. He announced to his Sentry to let him in.

The military advisor entered and bowed.

Nero was so excited he could not contain himself. "I've been waiting with delight. Do tell me your plan. Tell me every detail."

The Military Advisor nodded and proceeded to speak his plan.

"Oh Prefect, the most wonderful god of Rome, to lure the enigma into the city you shall decree with pomp and zeal that thousands of followers are in our prisons awaiting to be tortured in the grandest performance of all time, in the history of Rome's Circus."

"Can we, can we?" squealed Nero.

The advisor nodded, "You shall boastfully announce the date and time. The elite of Rome shall clamor about the event and he will hear of this and arrive to save the followers."

Nero touched his empty patch on his hair where his lock had been cut by the whizzing dagger. "How is this good for Rome?"

"When he comes, he will come with only a few men. There is no way he would be permitted an army into the Circus let alone the city of Rome. It is then that we shall capture him. We now know what he looks like and we will have spies throughout all of Rome seeking him. When we find where he is in the city, we capture him and torture and kill the enigma in the Circus for all to see."

"Yes, yes…he is not as strong when alone. I saw that with my own eyes."

The Military advisor was relieved that Nero loved his plan.

"We must allow time for the news of the festivities to reach him."

"Yes, yes, we must allow time for him to hear of this and arrive!" Nero agreed. "But, how shall we insure that he comes?"

"To lure him in, we shall raze villages and arrest every follower of the way and hold them in our prisons until the event. Word shall go out that we are gathering a feast for the lions, elephants, and hyenas. We tell of fantastic torturous events and competitions in the arena between beast and the follower zealots. The entire populace of Rome will lust to watch this spectacular event and to place lotteries on their beast of choice."

"Oh this is splendid indeed!" clapped Nero. "Say no more. It shall be done. Go do this now!"

The advisor was relieved that Nero had liked and agreed to his plan.

"Prefect, Sir, I will personally attend to the matter."

"Yes, yes! And I will dress as a god adorned with gold from head to foot."

The advisor nodded. "If it so pleases my god, I shall go now and attend to this matter."

"Go. Go!" exclaimed Nero excitedly, "There is much to do."

The advisor bowed and turned to leave.

Nero called out to him, "Make certain you announce that I shall open with a theatrical recital … one of Homer's best or shall I open with one of my own? Oh tell them it will be a surprise~"

"Yes, Prefect, I shall do that."

The Advisor left and Nero jumped up with glee and began to prance around trying out his dramatic opening prose and movements.

He suddenly halted, very pleased with himself and proclaimed, "Oh this will be remembered and written in the annals of all time! The day Nero slayed the Enigma!"

BAD NEWS ARRIVES

Some time had passed and refugees began coming to Cappadocia in larger numbers. They brought with them woeful tales of brutal attacks, torturous deaths and villages burned to the ground. Great numbers of innocent followers had been captured and drug away to Nero's prisons. The news of Caesar's plans to hold a massive persecution in the Circus Maximus had reached throughout the land.

People were fleeing their villages ahead of time out of fear they would be next, even those who weren't Followers of the Way. Longinus and the village workers were getting stressed on where to put them all, and feeding them was beginning to dwindle their store houses.

Longinus was now more cautious than ever to protect the hidden passageways from strangers who would sell such information for a silver coin. His biggest fear was for Rome to find out that his village was a refuge for followers and all those rescued from Roman prisons.

With village raids getting closer and closer to Cappadocia, he knew his village was also at high risk for Roman invasion and had his own set of personal fears.

Longinus, had grown fond of Priscilla, and worried for her safety more than any of the others. He depended greatly on her for advice just like he had with Mary.

Priscilla was now the most special person in his life. He told Khalid many times that if something ever happened to her, he would not be able to bear it. Khalid had always reassured him that she was safe and well.

It was a little while after the morning meal and Longinus heard people arguing. He looked over and saw Philip and Priscilla trying to calm down two men who were going at each other with harsh words. One of them was a newcomer to the village. He walked over to see what their heated conversation was about.

A man named Shalanum, who had arrived a few days before was arguing about the teachings of Simon the Magnus with a

Follower of the Way named Amanu. Philip and Priscilla were trying to reason with them both.

Shalanum argued, "He is the head apostle, anointed by Jesus; not a sorcerer!"

Amanu argued back, "He's a no good Samaritan conjuring demonic powers to do his miracles and wonders. John was there when he tried to buy the Apostleship from Peter. Both denied him it – but he did it any way for fame and greed. He is a liar and a deceiver. Peter told him he had no PART, nor LOT to be an apostle!"

Philip, who is always slow to anger, was outraged, "Jesus chose his apostles when he returned after his death on the cross and Simon the Magnus was not, nor ever has been one of them. Peter said Simon was in the gall of bitterness, he was a poison! He knew he was of the bonds of corruption and lawlessness and a viper in the path of the true word of God!"

Shalanum was not giving in, "You say such things because Simon undermined Mary of Magdalene and her ministry telling others she had no business teaching and not to listen to her for she is pagan. You know he is right. Women are to be silent and not teach to men!"

That was the wrong thing to say to Philip, he shouted back, "Samaritans call themselves the people of the true God, but they follow Simon their priest who practices Baal. Now he has blinded the people with lies of Babylon and tied his lies to Jesus the Messiah. He is of the devil teaching his own perversions, and Rome applauds him."

Amanu jumped in, "He uses the Master's name to exploit his pagan abominations! He has fueled the fires of Nero with his false teachings proclaiming the Followers are Jewish zealots spreading lies. He's called us rebels and turned God's word into a scroll of blasphemy!"

Shalanum made a fist and yelled, ""He is the Great One" -- a god. If it were not so, Rome would not have honored him as one with a statue on the Tiber between the bridges!"

Amanu fired back at him, ""Romans are bewitched by him! Simon appeases them pretending to worship Diana, when he secretly worships Semiramis in the form of Venus, his Babylonian Queen of Heaven! He is a sorcerer first and will never change!"

Longinus stood there listening to all these things not knowing what to do. His head would go from one to the other watching their angry faces as they shouted all these things.

Philip snapped at Shalanum, "He was never a part of the WAY, never! And now, look what he's done in Rome – he has corrupted the word of God and started his own idol worship claiming to be an Apostle of the Master and those of the Way as liars. Ohh….my anger boils at this one!"

Priscilla chimed in soft but firm, "This WOMAN will speak now. Peter said Simon is of Satan and one of those the Master warned of that was to come and twist his words saying, I am the real way, follow me. He is a harlot in purple robes whoring against the Master and the Father."

Philip looked Shalanum in the eye and spoke very direct, "I fear a great false church is emerging to dig its heels into the necks of the true Apostles and the teachings of the Way. Why else would Romans yell death to the followers while praising the Magnus with fame and coin?"

Shalanum looked puzzled at that and thought a moment. Priscilla saw him waver and seized the opportunity to counter.

"Is it not true that he is saying there is no more Law of Moses, only the teachings of Jesus and those he has changed to serve himself even declaring he is the son of God and now the God of the earth? Is it not so that he has declared for all to call him the Father as though he were God? And his followers have it so?"

Shalanum looked at Priscilla and asked sincerely, "Why would he say such things if they were not true?"

Priscilla answered him, "He is a greedy wolf that worships the one who gives him his magic. And his magic is not of the Father, not of Jesus. His reputation grows and people believe for they have no eyes to see or ears to hear. He has no gifts of God, only sorcerer's magic and a smooth tongue that speaks of his own customs and doctrine of devils calling themselves Christians after the manner of those in Antioch. He claims to be the anointed apostle to all the gentiles and people blindly follow him!"

Amanu, "He could never get away with such lies to the Jews nor Followers of the Way. I am sad he has bewitched you."

Shalanum was beginning to reason, "Where are such words of the Master to be found, that I can see with my own eyes?"

Philip answered, "I have scrolls that you can read in the sanctuary cave. Amanu, can you take him and show him?"

Amanu nodded and turned to Shalanum, "Come. Your eyes shall see the words of the Master. Then you can decide if it is or is not the same teaching."

Shalanum went with Amanu and Priscilla called to him, "Shalanum."

He stopped and turned around.

"You have free will to choose who you shall follow. No one here is making you choose. We only defend our Master's teachings and those of the Father."

Shalanum answered, "I want to follow the true way of the Master. I shall look at these scrolls and see."

Longinus became angry at hearing all of this, "I knew not of these dangerous things. I will kill this Simon."

Philip cautioned him, "You cannot kill him and think this will all end. Another will arise in his place. This is prophecy. It has been foretold to come. Jesus said if anyone says to you, 'Look, here is the Messiah!' or, 'Look, He is there!' do not believe it. He told us this would be. He said false Messiahs and false prophets will rise and show signs and wonders to deceive even the elect. It is now here."

Longinus angry and confused, "I never understand why we are to have evil all around us and no peace. This makes no sense."

Philip answered, "The Master showed us what must come to pass. He said fear not when you see these things, but to know he is with us even to the end. It is all a part of drinking from his cup."

"Then, I am glad I did not drink of that cup. I will not allow these things to be," snarled Longinus.

Philip saw that Longinus was again confused and tried to help him understand the mission of the Followers of the Way.

"If God had no purpose for us here he would have taken us straight to heaven. Instead, he left us with a gift of inner peace, and his Grace that will strengthen us through the struggles in this evil world. For we do the work of the Father for his other sheep who are not of this flock and who are yet to come into this evil world. To drink of his cup is to do as he did for his sheep."

Longinus dug his heels in against the words of Philip, "Evil men like Simon are worse than Nero! They kill with words instead of swords! They should all be slain!"

"You cannot fight the destiny of the world. You can only struggle with your own. Stand for God's truth and let him lead you where to go and do his will not yours."

Longinus was very frustrated at hearing what he considered more riddles, "You make no sense. You let me fight the Romans, if it protects the followers. Then you say I cannot fight this Simon who is a devil of Rome who hurts the followers."

Priscilla spoke up in a soothing voice to reason with Longinus, "Longinus, Simon was NEVER an apostle of the Messiah. But you can't kill everyone who does not believe or teaches another doctrine. Only God can judge, and he will."

Longinus paused and thought how much she sounded like Mary and Mary was always right about such things, so he calmed down.

"I do not understand these ways, but you do. So I will do as you say."

Longinus turned to Philip, "Why did Mary never tell me of these things?"

Philip, "Perhaps she did but because your ears were closed as they are now you did not hear it."

"What I hear always makes no sense."

Philip tired from this arguing sighed, "You will hear when you are ready."

Philip could see the disappointment on Longinus's face.

"What I spoke was not meant to trouble you, but to help."

"Why is this that you know these things and I do not?"

Philip put his hand on Longinus's arm, "God has called you for his purpose. It is he you must ask for understanding."

Longinus remembered the bellowing voice saying to him, how can I help you, when you do not seek me, nor listen to those I have sent before you and how he lay in the dust and admitted to the voice that this was true.

"I know him and I struggle with his way always."

Philip smiled softly, "Your eyes and ears are opening. Ask of him what you are to do and where you are to go."

"But I cannot drink of his cup as you do."

Philip answered, "Each have different gifts. You know how to battle and the cunning of Romans comings and goings. You are a heroic warrior, like Samson. I know nothing of how to battle. My gift is to teach the followers the Way and know well their confusion. We each serve a different purpose. God well knows this and provides us what we need, in his timing."

"Then I will drink of the cup he gave to me."

Priscilla smiled, "There is yet much to do. I must go and help the others."

They all departed and went about their duties.

A little while later…

It was early afternoon and Longinus and Khalid were outside having a serious talk on the safety of their village. They had been looking over the area making plans of how to hide more people in the underground passages.

"We have storages enough for now, but with these larger numbers we will run out fast. We need more grains, more cloth, more…oh Khalid we must stop this madness all together."

Khalid nodded his head. "We cannot wait to the day they do this evil. We must make a plan to free the followers from the prisons and stop this madness of Nero!"

"I agree. There is no time to waste. It will take us time to journey there. We must leave at dawn."

Khalid questioned, "Dawn?"

"Yes. With their soldiers out hunting down followers and burning villages, now is the best time to strike them."

Khalid, "We need to plan first. We don't just march there without a plan."

"We will plan as we go. The journey is far."

Khalid answered, "Then we leave at dawn. I will alert the men."

Longinus left to gather his weapons and armor. As he searched through a wall mounted with hasta's looking for the right one, he thought of his spear and regretted not having it.

He recalled the first time he broke his spear and the day he took it to a blacksmith in Joppa to mount it to a new shaft. That day he reared his horse and shouted to the Blacksmith, *the day will come when kings will seek the power that lies in this spear.* And how the blacksmith retaliated with the words, *you are too proud of another man's work.* And how he spoke back, *another man's work indeed. It is now my destiny!*

"Why must I always act on impulse?" he moaned. "The spear was given to me to wield. It was my destiny."

The next morning...

It was early dawn and the band of men had mounted their horses and were ready to head to Rome. There were a large number of them. Longinus looked over at Armond who had two men with him. Longinus wondered at this and went over to them.

"Who are these men?"

Armond answered, "My friends from Armenia have come to join us."

The two men looked at Longinus and nodded. Longinus gave them a cold stare then looked at Armond.

"Very well."

Longinus mounted his horse and rode over to Khalid.

"We need to keep our eyes on Armond and his friends."

"My same thoughts and Vitali's as well."

The army of men rode out.

BETRAYED

After a long journey, Longinus and his men had reached the outskirts of Rome. They made camp for the night and Longinus was going over their strategy on how they would enter Rome to free the followers from Nero's prison cells. Khalid, who was keeping a close eye on Armond, looked around and noticed that Armond and his friends were nowhere to be seen.

Longinus was focused on the plans. "This should all go well. We will enter Rome just before dawn."

Khalid stood up and looked out over the men. "Has anyone seen Armond?"

The men look around at each other. They chattered amongst themselves, and no one had seen him or his friends for quite a while. Some said they had not seen them since late afternoon. Others said they never entered the camp.

Longinus gave Khalid a serious look. "I have a feeling they may have went on to Rome; and not to save followers."

Khalid was very troubled, "Looks to me he goes to earn a bounty."

Longinus shared Khalid's concern. "If they have gone to warn Nero that we are here, we will do best to leave this camp and ready ourselves to attack."

Khalid cautioned, "We would be wise to move out now."

Longinus agreed with Khalid and directed the men to pull up camp. They quickly moved out and staked a position closer to the city. They readied themselves into attack positions. They watched and waited.

Meanwhile in Rome...

Armond and his two Armenian friends had quietly entered the city of Rome. It is dark outside and the streets are empty of people. There were fewer soldiers than usual keeping watch over the city and the ones they spotted looked tired and half asleep. It was just as Longinus had predicted, the largest number of soldiers were out on village raids.

Armond chuckled deviously under his breath, "It would have been a successful night for him. Now isn't that just too bad."

Armond and his two friends were carrying large bundles that look like wrapped wares for market. They secretly slithered along the sides of the buildings with their bundles and were careful to stay in the shadows.

They made haste to the Circus Maximus, the famous coliseum where all of Rome, and its' elite watched gladiator's battle to the death, beast hunts, chariot races and now it prided itself as the favorite den of torture for Followers of the Way. Its massive U-shaped structure measured 600 meters in length and 225 meters in width, and stood 100 feet tall. It allowed seating for over 250,000 citizens of Rome.

Armond and his friends found their way to a secluded entrance avoiding the main gates to the north, as that was guarded. They carefully broke the lock and lifted up the heavy beam that secured the gate and quietly made their way inside. Once inside they carefully closed the gate behind them.

Inside the Circus they opened their bundles and pulled out jugs of Greek Fire, a highly flammable liquid that was almost impossible to put out, for even water set it to blaze. They also pulled out bundles of unlit torches.

The three of them strategically went about spreading the Greek fire on the walls of the wooden shops that lined the bottom of the track of this massive structure and on everything made of wood they could find in the stadium. They moved very quickly with stealth, each one dousing a different area within the Circus. They moved rapidly up and down the corridors and into the stands spreading Greek fire here and there as they went.

All was going as planned until Armond passed by an iron barred gate and hungry lions lunged at the bars roaring at him with saliva dripping from their angry jaws. In the scare of it, he reacted impulsively and threw Greek fire at their faces; in a flash their jaws were set ablaze. The flames shot up fast engulfing the entire cage and spread fast to the adjacent ones, the caged animals went crazy as the inferno spread. Armond ran from there as fast as he could.

The others saw the blaze through the dark and took it as a signal to light their torches to set the fire. So they did. Within seconds the Greek Fire ignited along the walls and followed along rapidly like a slithering snake, whipping up into the rows of towering seats in the coliseum.

Armond and the others ran as fast as they could to flee the Circus Maximus. They barely got to through the gate when the entire Circus exploded into a roaring inferno everywhere at once. The flames furiously lapped upward, ominously blazing in the night sky. Their ears were dulled by its' deep, resonating thunder that grew louder and louder.

Armond motioned for them to split up and each went to a different district lighting every wooden building they found with their torches. Armond headed for the slums near the Palatine Hills setting the entire district to blaze. He reached the end of an alley way and threw his last torch, then ran out into the street. Gasping, he leaned against a wall, panting heavily, covering his face trying to catch his breath through the thick black smoke.

He watched as people came out of their homes panicked about the fire. The streets quickly filled with women and children shrieking and crying, running unsure of where to flee. Men fought desperately to douse the flames to no avail. Women shielded their children so they would not be trampled by the hoards fleeing from the flames, but many were tread down in spite of their effort.

Armond started running frantically about the city acting as though he was just as shocked of the fire as the others.

Roman citizens and soldiers battled the blazes with buckets of water that only kindled the flames to shoot up higher. Everything continued to burn faster and more furious. The winds picked up and rolled the whipping flames deeper into the city.

Armond ran up to a group of men in the street, "I saw who started the fire! It was the man they call the enigma and his followers!"

"I'll kill them for this!" shouted an angry man.

A soldier heard and grabbed Armond by the arm, "Where are they?"

Armond answered, "I saw them over there near the stables. They can't run far. I heard one say they would meet in the outskirts, outside the city."

Back at the outskirts waiting in the cliffs...

Khalid and Longinus watched the orange flaming sky and smoke bellowing up from the city. The evening starlit horizon was now a beacon of orange light. In the distance, shouts and screams were faintly heard among the crackling of the fiery inferno as it blazed.

Longinus shouted, "Rome is burning to the ground!"

Khalid added, "Do they burn followers or themselves?"

Longinus answered, "This is not good. We must leave. I have a feeling Armond is behind this."

"My feeling is the same," Added Khalid.

Longinus and Khalid watched as the fire continued to rise in the distance. They were mesmerized by its' magnitude as it rapidly spread across the night sky.

Khalid started to move out, "I'll signal the men."

"Wait. Do not signal the men. No soldiers will be coming for us when Rome is burning to the ground," Longinus paused to think, then said, "We watch to see if Armond and his friends return to our old camp. I will take some men. You stay here."

Khalid nodded and Longinus left to gather a band of his men to return with him to the outskirt and their old campsite to wait and watch for Armond and his two friends.

Meanwhile, back in the streets of Rome...

Armond overheard a Centurion tell the guard that he was leaving for Antium to alert Nero of the fire. Armond quickly ran to the side of the Centurion's horse and grabbed the bridle.

"I saw who started the fire. It was the man they call the enigma and his band of followers."

The Centurion looked Armond sternly in the eye as he tried to keep his spooked horse steady. "Is that all?"

"I heard him boast as the fire burned that Nero will have no Circus for his grand performance to kill the thousands of followers."

"You heard him say that did you?"

"I did."

The Centurion felt a wave of relief and was glad to have something to tell Nero for the account of the fire.

"Thank you good man, I will tell Nero of your account."

The Centurion rode out of the burning city. Armond motioned for his friends to follow him. They followed Armond to their horses and found them spooked by the fire. They reared up and whinnied wildly, snorting through the smoke as they desperately fought to break free. The whites of their bulging eyes were glazed over with fear.

Armond and his men draped the horse's eyes with blankets and led them away from the burning buildings.

People were running in all directions screaming and shielding their heads from flying lit ashes. They trampled one another as they frantically searched for a way out. Many were hit from falling debris and burned to death in the street. The horrifying sounds of shrill cries and wailing screeches filled the air.

Armond and his men finally led their horses outside of the burning part of the city. They mounted their steeds and rode wildly out toward the outskirts.

Back at the camp site...

Longinus and his men were in the shadows waiting for Armond to return to the campsite. They heard horses approaching. Longinus looked and it was Armond and his friends. They were lying in wait silently ready to ambush them.

Armond walked his horse around the deserted camp and was surprised that no one was there. He moved about slowly through the empty camp checking things out.

"They have gone," said Armond.

His Armenian friend added, "One of their scouts must have told them Rome was burning and they left."

Armond got down from his horse and went over to the fire. He knelt down and felt the ashes.

"They left before we started the fire."

"Do you think they followed us?" asked his friend.

Armond answered, "I think they knew we left and went into the city to find us. I wonder how much they know?" He peered toward the shadows as though he sensed someone was there.

Longinus motioned for the others to make their move. Immediately daggers were hurled hitting the legs of the Armenians and Armond. They fell to the ground screaming in pain.

Armond drew his sword and a dagger sliced through his fingers; sending his sword and two fingers flying in the air. Armond wailed out.

Longinus shouted from the shadows, "Throw all your weapons in the fire pit or more daggers will fly!"

All of them quickly threw their weapons in the fire pit. Longinus and his men stepped out from the shadows.

"So you have set Rome on fire? Why?"

Armond clutched his hand to stop the bleeding from his severed fingers. He answered as he winced with pain.

"Why not? Rome has burned enough of our cities to the ground and killed thousands of our people."

Longinus was silent as he tried to reason what Armond had just said.

Nervously Armond continued, "The Parthians are just as bad. They act as our friends and stab us in the back as well as their own people."

Longinus cut a strip of cloth from his tunic and tossed it to Armond.

"Tie your hand to stop the bleeding.

Armond tied his hand while Longinus thought of what he should do.

As Armond winced and moaned over the loss of his fingers Longinus approached him. He stood, towering over him with a stern face.

"Hate and greed for power rule this world."

Armond looked up surprised and curious at what Longinus spoke. Longinus continued, "We will take you back to Cappadocia to heal. If no further trouble, you will be free to return to Armenia."

Armond knew what Longinus meant is that if he was found lying he would be dealt with. He remembered the Parthian's words that Longinus hated and killed liars.

Longinus turned to the men and ordered them to bind the Armenians with rope around their waist and necks. He watched until this was done then mounted his horse and ordered the men to do the same.

The wounded Armenians struggled to mount and Longinus designated two strong loyal men to help them up on their horses and hold onto each of their ropes. He was not going to be tricked by any of them again.

Being captured was not a part of Armond's plans. He made eye contact with the two Armenians as though he were telepathically giving them a message. He then shouted to Longinus.

"There were no thousands of followers in the prison."

"What did you say?" queried Longinus.

"In the fire, I watched soldiers open the prisons and there were less than a hundred that ran out."

Longinus said no more and gave the motion to ride out. Armond looked disgusted as though that had not gone as he planned.

They travel a short distance and Armond gave a nod to the bound Armenian to his left. He then fell forward on his horse as though he had passed out. The Armenian called out, "Armond has died."

Khalid rode over and touched his neck for a pulse.

"He's not dead."

The Armenian pleaded, "He will die from the loss of blood."

Longinus looked over at Armond. He rode over to Khalid, "I do not want this man to detain us."

Khalid answered, "Leave him and let a few of the men attend to him until he can ride."

The Armenian friend yelled out, "He needs a physician. He suffers years now from an issue of blood. It's not the severed fingers."

Longinus turned to the other Armenian, "Is this true?"

The Armenian nodded, "He knows death is at his door. This is why he is reckless in his vengeance."

Khalid whispered to Longinus, "If this is true, he's best to die in the outskirts. Not in Cappadocia."

"Perhaps," Longinus paused for a moment. "Untie the Armenian and Armond. Give them rations and leave them."

The men untied the Armenian and took Armond down from his horse and laid him on the ground. Longinus watched as the other Armenian winced with pain holding his wounded leg and hobbled over to the passed out Armond.

Longinus ordered, "Stay with him and bring him back to us when he is better. Return whether he lives or dies or your friend will be put to death."

The Armenian nodded his head in agreement. Longinus directed his men to continue toward Cappadocia.

The Armenian sat next to Armond's body until the band of men were out of site. He nudged Armond's body and Armond sat straight up and spoke.

"Now we ride to Antium,"

ANTIUM THEATER

The Centurion reached Antium in record time to give Nero the account of Rome's burning, but Nero was not eager to hear it. The Centurion was frustrated that with such a vital matter, Nero was putting his performance first and not concerned with the Burning of Rome. He would finish before he heard any of it.

"Guard, show the Centurion where he can stand to watch my performance. Make sure he has a good view."

The Centurion responded back, "But Prefect, Sir…"

Nero interrupted, "We'll speak of the fire after my performance. Do you not agree that is the best thing to do?"

The Centurion nodded, "Prefect, Sir, where shall you have me stand?"

"Guard, tend to the matter," stated Nero as he dramatically flung his arm out toward the stage, "My audience awaits."

Nero pranced out to the main stage and the audience cheered.

The Guard locked eyes with the Centurion as if to signal a shared empathy for Nero's insanity. None the less, he led him close to the stage, next to the backstage curtain, making sure he had a good view of Nero's performance.

The Centurion stood in the wings of the stage impatiently watching as Nero sang the song of the destruction of Troy. He worried over the insanity of it all. Nero, he thought, was a mad man unfit to rule.

Finally the performance ended, but his final bows and accolades seemed to last longer than the play itself.

Nero eventually made his way back stage in a state of euphoria, high on the standing ovations and gleaming with joy.

Nero addressed the Centurion with glee.

"Did you like my performance?"

"Of course Prefect, Sir. Now…"

Nero interrupted, "What part was your favorite?"

"Prefect Sir, Rome is …"

Nero in his own self- absorbed state cuts him off again and asks, "Was it the song?"

"Yes, Prefect, Sir it was the song. Now an urgent matter has…"

"What part of the song?"

"Prefect, Sir, Rome is burning as we speak by the hands of the Enigma and his Followers of the Way."

"This fire… is it raging or just a little thing?"

"Prefect, Sir, it is seen in the sky from the outskirts of Antium!"

"Then there is no need to return immediately. Let the guards put it out before their god returns."

"Prefect, it is burning to the ground."

"If it does, then I shall build another and have it named after their god. It shall be called Nero."

After speaking those words with the facial expression of a crazed idiot, Nero, motioned his guards.

"I'm ready to be escorted to my quarters," He looked at the Centurion and added, "Now run along, and bother me no more this night."

The Centurion was left standing alone. He shut his eyes tight and cringed at the lunacy of it all.

Later, inside his quarters, Nero watched from the window of his opened portico the burning of Rome. He stood hypnotized watching the orange tongues of blazing fire, far off in the distant night sky.

After a long while, he suddenly got an urge to pour himself a drink of wine and boldly toasted himself to a fake audience in his empty quarters.

"To Nero the highest God of Rome and of all the World!"

He drank it all down at once then filled it again. He went to the portico and looked out again.

He held out his goblet and recited, "Thus in their town and o'er them anguished grief, hovered dark-winged as though that very day all Troy with shrieks were crumbling down with fire."

He turned and arrogantly pranced about his quarters holding high his wine goblet toasting himself as he sang just as off key as he did in the theater, *"Rouse, you horse-taming Trojans! Break the wall of the Argives and fling among the ships, wondrous blazing fire…"*

Hitting a shrill, high note, he thrust his arm out to make a dramatic gesture and spilled red wine all over his prized zebra skinned rug.

He abruptly stopped singing and knelt down on the zebra skin. He hurriedly wiped away at the wine with his hand smearing it more. Disgusted, at the horrible mess, he angrily tipped his goblet dumping the rest of the wine out shaking it fiercely, then threw the empty goblet down hard.

"I'll just have to get another," He said soothingly to himself about the rug, and the wine."

Unexpectedly, there was a knock at the door.

"What do you want?" shouted Nero.

A Sentry answered through the closed door, "Prefect, Sir. A man named Armond stated that you wished to see him. He looks like a Parthian. Should I send him away?"

"Let him in."

"Prefect, Sir, the door is bolted from the inside."

"Very well," sighed Nero as he went to the door and unbolted it. "Now send him in."

"The Sentry opened the door and a disheveled, Armond with a wrapped hand entered.

The Sentry asked, "Prefect, Sir, should I stay?"

"Run along. There is no need to stay."

The Sentry gave Armond a stern look and left. The door no sooner shut and Nero addressed Armond.

"From reports, I trust I supplied enough Greek fire. Did you find all the torches? Speak! I want to hear all the details!"

Meanwhile in the outskirts of Rome ...

Longinus and the band of men are now far from Rome. They are galloping with good stride and Longinus raised his arm and signaled the men to stop. As the men slowed, Longinus shouted, "We stop here and rest our horses."

As the men came to a stop, Khalid rode over to Longinus with a very disturbed look on his face.

"There's a feeling inside me that Armond deceived us more than we know."

"I have the same feeling. I now doubt that he could not travel."

Longinus looked at the men. They were tired and hungry. Their horses were as well. He looked up at the evening sky and over at Khalid who too was weary.

"Men, make camp. We rest for the night and leave at early dawn."

The men dismounted and started to make camp.

Back at Antium in Nero's quarters...

Armond had just finished telling Nero all the details of burning Rome.

"Tell me the part again where you went to the Centurion and told him you heard the Enigma bragging. I like that part!"

Armond, now dull of repeating everything over and over to amuse Nero was eager to get his reward and leave.

"The rumors were truly spread to your liking. Now, can we settle the matter of my bounty?"

Nero was not accustomed to anyone who did not entertain his whims, and he certainly had no tolerance for anyone asking for their pay before he was ready to give it. To make it worse for Armond, Nero was not happy with him for ending the playful conversation he was so enjoying. His pleasant countenance changed instantly into that of an angry man.

"I must reconsider the matter."

"Reconsider? All was done as you asked."

"Ah, but now with the fire the citizens will be in distress. Rome will be without taxes on many things. Lost buildings, dead livestock, and the dead…oh the dead…they will never again pay a tax."

Armond looked down at his bandaged hand and tried to control his own anger that was welling up inside.

Nero continued, "Funds will be needed to rebuild Rome."

"Prefect, you made a deal."

"A deal?"

"Do you want a reputation for not honoring your deals? No bounty hunter will work for you again." Snapped Armond.

Nero was livid at the gal of Armond to dare say such a thing.

"Reputation? Are you ready to have the reputation of the one who burned Rome to the ground?"

Armond realized he went too far with his words to Nero. He fidgeted with his bandage to self-calm.

"I am just saying a god always rewards his servants when they obey."

Nero became less ruffled at hearing those words.

"Indeed. Therefore, your reward shall be that I will not kill you for burning Rome."

Armond was furious but controlled his temper and held back his tongue. He bowed and turned to leave. As he approached the door, Nero asked, "By the way, what happened to your hand?"

"Burned it lighting the fire."

Nero smiled as the whites of his eyes bulged all around like that of a crazed man. The look sent chills down Armond's back, he hurried out.

Outside the door, the Sentry was standing guard and stared sternly at Armond.

"What are you looking at?" sneered Armond as he passed.

RETURN TO CAPPADOCIA

After a long journey, Longinus and his band of men finally entered his village in Cappadocia. Priscilla was passing out food and saw them returning. She ran to greet them.

As Longinus dismounted his horse, he saw Priscilla running toward him. His heart was filled with joy at the sight of her smile. She dropped her basket of bread and leaped at him and he caught her up in an embrace.

"Oh, I have worried so for you," She said.

"And I longed for this embrace."

"Did you free the followers from the prison?"

Longinus loosed his embrace and held Priscilla by her shoulders in front of him. He looked into her eyes and spoke in a very concerned tone, "This was another one of Nero's traps. There were no thousands of followers."

"I don't understand? The villages? The refugees said Rome took their people hostage?"

"They took no hostages. Roman soldiers let some escape knowing they would believe the others were taken hostage like in the past. Instead they were massacred and burned with their villages. It is me he wants."

Priscilla's countenance fell hearing this.

"Three of our new men burned the city. I fear Nero will blame us for it."

"Why did you let your men set the fires?"

"Not our men, it was Armond and his Armenian friends that did so. But, I fear we will be blamed."

As they were talking, one of the newly recruited Parthian bounty hunters approached Longinus.

"I heard the Parthians set Rome a blaze."

Longinus gave the man a curious stare, "Parthians?"

"I want you to know, we had nothing to do with Armond or the fire."

Longinus quipped back, "He said he and his friends were Armenian."

"He lied."

"It's bold of you to report this. Why did you not tell me before?"

"We did not know he lied until Khalid said it was Armond the Armenian bounty hunter who started the fire."

"Why should I trust you speak the truth?"

"We fight Rome. It is our enemy, same as yours."

"You have shown this to be true. Well done."

The man nodded and left. Longinus watched him as he walked away. He looked at Priscilla and asked, "Can a Parthian be trusted?

Priscilla took Longinus by the hand.

"Come and eat," she said as she led him away, "You must be hungry."

Sometime later...

It was now dusk and Longinus and Priscilla were still seated in the Dining hall. Almost everyone had left. Priscilla was telling wonderful stories and Longinus was enjoying every word she told.

"Then Mary picked up the bowl of soup from in front of the lazy man, and said – if you will not work then you shall not eat. The man jumped right up and went out and started chopping the wood!"

Longinus and Priscilla laughed.

"I can see Mary doing that!" He tried to stop laughing to talk, "She always had a way of getting people's attention!"

Longinus looked around the dining hall at the few who were still eating. He stood up and smiled at Priscilla.

"Come. Let us look at the stars and see what they have to tell us."

Priscilla got up and they walked outside toward the stone fence that surrounded the garden. Longinus leaped over it and turned around, "Come, leap, I'll catch you."

Priscilla looked to the side and took three steps and walked through a small opened gate. Longinus looked surprised. "There is a gate?" They both laughed.

They walked along and found a secluded spot.

"This looks good," said Longinus, "Come we sit here."

Longinus nestled in on the grass and lay on the ground on his back with his knees bent looking up at the sky. Priscilla sat on the ground next to Longinus and looked up at the stars.

"Your neck will sore. Come," he patted the ground.

Priscilla smiled and lay on her back next to Longinus.

"This is much better," she said softly.

In the distance, the chimney rocks make a silhouette against the moonlit sky. The tops appeared to glow a deep yellow orange.

They lay nestled together looking up at the stars. It was a moment Longinus had dreamed of having and now he was living it. He did not want it to end.

Longinus had something on his heart that he wanted to ask Priscilla, but did not know how to approach it. For now he was content just to be with her alone in the garden. He cherished the moment. Then after a little while longer his heart beat stronger for her and he grew anxious of asking his question.

Longinus took in a deep breath of night air and let it out slowly, "At night when we are at camp, I look at the stars and wonder what they know of destiny."

"I know Abraham read the stars…and so did the prophets. They tell of what is to come."

"And what do they tell you tonight?"

Priscilla thought a moment, then answered, "They tell me my heart is growing fond of you."

Longinus smiled, "Look! That big star in the middle. Do you know what that tells me?"

"I am not sure. What does it tell you?"

"It tells me that what your little star has said is true."

Longinus turned gently and lifted up and leaned over Priscilla. He softly kissed her on the forehead.

"I grow tired of being alone. Will you share your life with me and wed me?"

Priscilla did not expect to hear that. She sat up and looked at Longinus surprised. Longinus blushed. He feared he had said the wrong thing.

Longinus quickly tried to back track, "I am sorry I …"

Priscilla interrupted. "Stop. I want you to know what you ask."

"I know what I ask. I ask you to be my bride!"

"You are always so impulsive. Is it the stars or the wine from supper that brings you to ask this?"

"I had only two cups of wine. I know what I ask."

"Do you? I will grow old. You may not. Is it possible for you to wed knowing this?"

"I more than any know this. Will you wed me?"

"Yes."

They embraced holding each other tight, not letting go for the longest time. Finally, they unlock and Longinus kissed her on the cheek. Priscilla returned him a kiss, not on his cheek but on his lips. They kissed passionately and a star shot across the sky.

"Look!" exclaimed Priscilla softly, "A shooting star!"

Longinus looked up, "The stars have indeed favored me this night."

THE DREAM VISION

That night Longinus could not sleep for thinking of Priscilla agreeing to wed him. He was so excited thinking of the day he would carry Priscilla over the threshold.

He tossed and turned then leaped out of bed to his bedroom door. He stood in the doorpost, turned around and positioned his arms in a gesture, pretending he was carrying Priscilla in his arms. He followed through the threshold. Not satisfied with how that felt, he shook his arms at his side and went back to the threshold, and tried it again. Still not satisfied, he threw his hands up in the air. Talking out loud to himself, he said,

"When that day comes I will know how to do it."

He climbed back into bed, tossed and turned some more and finally fell asleep.

He had a dream… Longinus was inside of Mary's tomb. He lifted the wooden lid of her coffin to see her again. Instead of Mary it was Priscilla. She handed him the spear head. He took it and when he did, Priscilla faded away and disappeared completely.

Longinus awoke and shot straight up in his bed, sweating profusely. Not knowing what to think of his dream he grew desperate. He leaped from his bed and paced the floor.

"Why do I always have haunting visions?" He ran out of the house in his tunic.

He found his way to Philip's home and banged persistently on his door, shouting his name.

Philip opened the door half asleep, "What is it? Are Romans coming?"

"Philip I must speak with you."

"Come in, we shall speak."

Longinus stepped inside and started to pace as he spoke, "I have had a haunting dream. But, first I must tell you, I asked Priscilla to wed me and she has agreed."

Philip looked surprised then listened very closely.

"In my dream I was inside of Mary's tomb. I lifted the coffin lid to see her one last time and it was Priscilla. She handed me my spear head and then she disappeared. What does this mean?"

Philip was bewildered.

"In this world of the flesh we are given but a fleeting moment of God's infinite measure of time. We must each use it wisely. Each has a destiny that will lead us home."

Philip pointed at a small wooden table with three stools around it. He motioned for Longinus to sit. As he sat down, Philip lit a candle and the dark room flickered making a mysterious dancing light.

Philip sat down across from Longinus and began to speak in a serious tone, "It seems a part of your destiny died with Mary. Priscilla has come into your life to hand that part back to you. But, she too shall pass on before you," Philip paused for a moment. "Are you ready to accept that part?"

"Priscilla said to me this night, I will grow old, you may not. Is it possible for you to accept? I told her yes."

"Know this Longinus, there is always another layer to a dream. The same as there is with the words of our Lord and the prophets. This is why things always look confusing until you are ready to see. When you are ready, you will see the next layer."

Longinus appeared torn and more confused than ever.

Philip asked, "Do you love her?"

Longinus answered, "Yes."

"Then wed her," smiled Philip.

Longinus returned the smile and walked to the door and went home with peace of mind and very happy.

FOUR YEARS LATER

Time had passed and it had now been four years since Longinus and Priscilla made their wedding vows. They have continued to help the Followers of the Way find refuge and in so doing suffered many hardships. But, the joy of a son, now age three, had kept their hearts filled with an ultimate richness money could never buy. They named him Justus. He was a handsome boy and quick to learn. He had Priscilla's eyes and the stubbornness of his father; always wanting to do things perfect the first time and frustrated when he couldn't.

Longinus and his band of men had continued their campaigns to rescue and avenge Followers of the Way from the hands of Roman soldiers.

Priscilla would endure long weeks and often months without Longinus at home, yet, she adjusted to that very well. Perhaps it was because suffering hardships had become a way of life, or perhaps it was because her heart was fixed on her life's purpose of serving the Lord and attending to the needs of others; she knew no other way. Life to her was a day to day blessing and she always had faith that Longinus would return safely. While he was away her heartfelt comfort was caring for and teaching Justus the ways of the Lord.

On this day, it had been several weeks since Longinus had left, and this time Priscilla was showing concern and wanting him home. She was about to give birth to their second child and longed for him to be there when the child was born. With every sound of horse's hooves she would look to see if it was him.

Even though she was about to deliver she was still performing duties to help others and was with Philip in the garden holding a basket as he filled it with fresh vegetables.

"I must be patient," said Priscilla to Philip, "All will be according to God. My mother would tell me, worry destroys the moment that God has blessed us with to do his will. Instead, you must pray."

"She was a blessed woman," Answered Philip.

"I wish Justus could have known her," She sighed.

Philip felt Priscilla's sadness and sought to comfort her, "He will know her love and kindness through you."

Priscilla touched her stomach, "My time is soon. I should not be so selfish with my own desires."

She watched as Justus stacked little rocks making a pretend stone wall around a wooden hand carved horse. "I am blessed with Justus and this new child. That is more than enough."

Not long after, horse's hooves were heard again. Priscilla looked out to see who approached. This time it was Longinus.

Justus looked up from his play. Excited he shouted, "Papa!" He and Priscilla ran to meet him as he dismounted his horse. Justus grabbed hold hugging Longinus's leg.

Longinus grabbed Justus up in the air and swung him on top of his shoulders. Justus hung onto Longinus's neck bellying out a child's gleeful laugh. Smiling, Longinus turned to Priscilla and embraced her with Justus laughing from on top of his massive shoulders.

He touched her belly, "I was afraid you might deliver while I was gone."

"My time is soon. Come, you must be hungry." They walk toward their house with Justus still on top of his shoulders.

Khalid had been watching from a distance and stood smiling. He looked down to Vitali, "He is a happy man. Good to see him so."

Vitali barked in agreement.

ARMOND RETURNS TO NERO

Meanwhile back in Rome, Armond had entered the city and was approaching the Palace of Nero. He dismounted his horse and felt the stubs on his hand that were once two fingers. His hatred for Nero had grown inside him like a festering sore.

He seethed under his breath, "A god?" He spat on the ground, "I shall see how he bleeds."

Armond approached the guard holding an ivory box.

"Please send word to Nero that Armond is here with a gift."

The guard seized the ivory box and opened the lid. Inside were two very large precious gems. The guard picked one up and held it up to the sun. It was crystal clear and glittered brightly.

"Be careful guard not to dull the shine with your fingers. Nero will not be pleased."

The guard put the gem back in the box and shut the lid. He gave it back to Armond.

"I'll tell him you are here."

"He will be very pleased," Said Armond, as he nodded.

The guard called for a Sentry. When the Sentry came he opened the lid to the ivory box and showed him the gift, then sent him to Nero with the message. Armond nodded to the guard and waited.

It wasn't long and the Sentry returned.

"Nero is excited to receive your gift. He will see you now."

The guard searched Armond to make sure he had no weapons. Finding none he motioned for him to follow the Sentry.

Armond followed him into the palace escorted by two guards, at his side.

The Sentry announced his arrival and he was received by Nero. The two guards led him in.

"Oh god of Rome, I had hoped to give you my gift privately. As I wish to beg pardon for past grievances and discuss possibility of future tasks."

Understanding that Armond meant the burning of Rome and definitely wanting to keep that a secret he ordered the guards to leave.

More eager to see the gems than to hear of further evil deals, Nero eagerly pleaded, "Now what did you bring me?"

"It is a wondrous surprise."

Clapping his hands rapidly together, Nero exclaimed, "Oh I do love surprises. Shall I close my eyes?"

"You must or you will ruin the surprise."

Nero giggled with glee and closed his eyes. Armond quickly opened a hidden compartment on the underside of the ivory box and pulled out a dagger. He quickly hid it inside his shirt. No sooner had he done so and Nero peeked through his eyes.

"No peeking," Stated Armond, "But I will let you hold the box and have you guess what is in it."

"Oh you do make this so fun!"

Armond gave Nero the ivory box cautioning once more, "Now no peeking as you guess."

Nero smiling with his eyes tightly shut took the box. Armond quickly pulled his dagger and lunged it at Nero's throat. He pressed it in deep and watched him gasp.

Nero dropped the ivory box and lifelessly fell forward against Armond's body. Holding the dagger in place, Armond drug Nero to his throne and struggled to place his body on it. With the dagger still tightly lodged inside his throat, he lifted Nero's lifeless hand and wrapped it around the dagger, making sure it looked as though he had killed himself.

As Armond turned to flee, the room suddenly began to rumble. The floor of the palace shook and Armond fell to the floor. He panicked as thoughts of whether Nero was or wasn't really a god filled his mind. He looked over at Nero's dead body on the throne.

"I am certain he is dead."

Suddenly the dead body shook and a demonic sorcerer dressed in a hooded cloak with the appearance of an old man, stepped out from Nero's body. He suddenly shapeshifted into a younger version of himself wearing an ornately decorated robe of an elite.

Armond cringed with fear.

The sorcerer glared at Armond and angrily shouted, "Do you realize what you have done?"

Armond turned to run and the Sorcerer pointed his finger, freezing Armond in time space. The Sorcerer spun around and around, gathering energy like a whirl wind. Armond's frozen body was pulled inside it and suddenly, they both disappeared.

The Sorcerer and a frozen Armond suddenly reappeared in what seemed to be a demonic Wizard's lair. The round cavern like chamber had a ceiling of great height that narrowed at the top. Rows of shelves filled the walls, full of jars labeled with odd ingredients like monkey eyes, ox brains, and mixed vials of potions and empty glass beakers. There were baskets of strange shaped roots, some were labeled and some not. Leather pouches filled with ground powder mixtures lay in rows between the baskets.

Ancient scrolls and codex's bound with animal hides and filled with spells lay stacked and scattered on a massive iron table in the center. Some were opened displaying horrid creatures and strange writings.

Off to the side, was the most troubling sight. Dark dried blood stains adorned an eerie throne made from the scull of a giant with the lower jaw cut off. Steps made from bones led up to an ominous seated throne imbedded deep inside the dark cavity of the skull's nose. Dragon's teeth protruded up from the floor encircling the sides and back of the skull, towering high above it. The pointed tips pierced into the highest point of the lair's ceiling.

Five dark tunnel openings were evenly spaced around the cavernous lair. A smoky red haze floated from one tunnel opening to another, crisscrossing into the formation of a sinister symbol of a five starred pentagram.

A menacing, evil foreboding permeated throughout the entire cavernous lair.

The Sorcerer hurriedly rummaged through his scattered codexes and found the one he sought. He swiped off a thick film of dust with the sleeve of his arm, then blew away the little that was left. He opened it and placed it before him on the iron table.

"I was in that body way too long," He looked over at the frozen Armond and noticed his face was frozen with a look of horror, he chuckled, "He actually did me a favor."

The sorcerer turned the pages in the book, quickly scanning in search of what he sought.

"Aha! Yes, here it is!"

His eyes shifted as he read line by line. He raised his hand and pointed to one of the leather pouches on the shelf. It floated swiftly through the air and stopped in front of him. He grabbed the pouch, opened it quickly and took a pinch of powder. He shoved the codex out of the way and placed the pinch of powder on the iron table in front of him. He began to chant...

"Oh powers of darkness return to me, show me the spear and its' destiny."

The strange powder turned into a fluid orb and floated up from the iron table growing bigger until it filled the room like a portal into time. The Sorcerer watched as a vision filled image manifested within the portal.

A sepulcher appeared with an ornate epitaph on the outside of it. It was that of Mary Magdalene. The sepulcher opened and inside was a wooden coffin. It glowed until it became transparent, leaving only the head of the spear to be seen.

The silhouette of a hand reached down and took away the head of the spear. The image dissolved and another manifested.

The spear was being remounted on a long strong shaft.

The image again dissolved and another appeared.

Longinus appeared wielding the spear victoriously.

The Sorcerer cringed and hissed, "Curses!" he shouted.

The vision dissolved and another appeared: *There were flashes of lightning and a succession of kings, each going into battle holding the spear. They all had blood red crosses on their banners.*

He watched as a series of visions presented the spear being stolen again and again. Each time a silhouette of a hand grabbed hold of the spear and a different king's face appeared.

He watched as each new King left the battlefield with great victory.

Without warning, the images dissolved and this time, so did the orb leaving the Sorcerer in a panic.

"The end, I must know the end!" The Sorcerer grabbed more powder and threw it on the iron table. He repeated the chant, "Oh powers of darkness return to me, show me the spear and its' destiny."

Again, the strange powder turned into a fluid orb and floated up from the iron table growing bigger until it filled the room like a portal into time. Inside the portal was another vision.

Time flashed forward and three different spears with three different owners appeared. Each owner claimed their spear was the one that possessed true power, yet, none of them could prove their spear held any power at all.

Suddenly there was a burst of light and the true spear appeared. It twirled around dancing in the air. Suddenly it spun around furiously and shot through a dark tunnel with lightning speed. It abruptly stopped suspended in mid-air in front of a mountain of rock not made from human hands, then vanished.

An angel walked out from the same mountain and over to another angel who was waiting. The first angel nodded. The other angel moved to the mountain's side, he folded his arms and stood guard with his legs a shoulder's width apart.

A strong, muscular Warrior King-like angelic figure appeared. He nodded to the angels standing guard.

Suddenly, the spear shot out from the mountain side with lightning speed and abruptly halted, mid-air in front of the Warrior King. The Warrior King laid his hand out, palm side up and the spear lowered itself into his palm. The Warrior King wrapped his strong hand around it and the spear glowed like a golden lightning rod.

The Warrior King peered up to the heavens and the deep pitch of a mighty trumpet sounded so loudly the orb burst, ending the vision.

"The only way to end such a mighty destiny is to hide the spear and make certain no one ever finds it," proclaimed the Sorcerer.

The Sorcerer turned toward Armond and looked at his outstretched hand with two missing fingers.

"Yes, yes. He will do anything to have those back."

The sorcerer raised his hand to undo the spell, and then hesitated, "I don't really desire to fool with him anymore."

He lowered his hand, and thought a moment, He shrugged his shoulders, then raised it again. "Not what I wanted, but, he will have to do."

He waved his hand and Armond unfroze.

Armond screamed and rattled off a myriad of questions, "What are you? What do you want? Where am I? What…"

The sorcerer waved his hand and Armond's mouth was gone. He had nothing to speak out of. Armond frantically felt at the place where his mouth once was. It was smooth and covered over with skin.

"Fools are better seen, and not heard. Now where was I?" The Sorcerer spun around and in a flash he and Armond disappeared in mid-air.

In an instant, the Sorcerer and Armond appeared in the South of France at the sepulcher of Mary Magdalene. Armond was fearful. The whites of his eyes showed all around. He was a very pitiful sight.

The Sorcerer addressed Armond in a tone indicating that he really could care less, "Now, I can restore your mouth and your fingers if you agree to steal something for me. Will you agree?"

Armond shook his head yes. The Sorcerer clicked his fingers. Instantly Armond's mouth and fingers reappeared. He felt his mouth and his new fingers.

"Now go inside and open the wooden coffin. Look beneath the robe and you will find the head of the spear. Take it and bring it back to me."

Armond broke open the sepulcher and went inside. Hesitating, he looked back at the Sorcerer. The Sorcerer raised his hand and gave him an angry stare. Armond quickly got back to doing what he was asked and made his way inside.

Once inside the sepulcher Armond looked around in fear. It was taboo in his culture to open any grave of the dead.

He slowly went over to the wooden coffin and worked to pry it open, shuddering the entire time. The lid finally came loose and he opened it up. He closed his eyes and dared not look upon the dead body for fear of a curse.

He clumsily felt for the robes edge and found it, then lifted it to feel for the head of the spear. He pricked his finger on its tip and winced. Keeping his eyes closed, he picked it up.

The finger miraculously healed itself in an instant but with his eyes closed he did not notice.

Armond closed the lid to the wooden coffin and quickly made his way out of the sepulcher, all the while he kept his eyes shut tight.

Armond held out the spear for the Sorcerer to take. The Sorcerer jerked back, hiding his face with his cloak he shouted, "Cover it you fool!"

"Armond quickly took off his outer vest and wrapped it around the spear. He curiously looked at his healed hand and wondered. He looked over at the shaken Sorcerer.

"You wanted it. What am I to do with it?"

"Hold it until I show you where to hide it."

The Sorcerer spun around and they both disappeared.

POOF! the two reappeared in Petra, Jordon just inside the sig.

Armond no sooner looked up at the ornate carvings of architecture in the mountain rock and the Sorcerer spun around again. They suddenly appeared deeper inside Petra. The Sorcerer looked around.

"Now, there it is," The Sorcerer pointed at a boulder and levitated it up and moved it forward, exposing a deep well.

"Throw it in the well and cover it with rock. Hurry."

Armond quickly threw the spear in the hole and tossed rock and stones over the top.

Watching closely the Sorcerer motioned for Armond to stop, "That will do." Still pointing, he levitated the boulder back in its place. It settled with a jolt.

"You have done well. But since you are a liar, a thief, and a deceitful man who cannot be trusted, I will…"

Armond interrupted pleading, "Please, I did all you asked."

"Yes, you did today. But, tomorrow you will tell of this for a price."

"I swear I will guard these secret things with my life."

"Very well then. So you shall."

"The Sorcerer locked eyes with Armond and his body trembled then solidified into stone.

With an evil grin, the Sorcerer admired Armond's new stone physic.

"This is one promise I know you shall keep."

BIRTH PAINS

Back in Cappadocia, Longinus was finishing dinner with his family and leaned back in his chair.

"Another meal fit for a king."

Priscilla smiled and was so happy to have her husband home. "You are the king of this house, just ask Justus."

Longinus looked over to Justus. "I am king of this house?"

"And mother a queen and me a prince," They all laughed at the thought of that.

Longinus put his elbow on the table and got down on his knees. "Come Justus. Let me see how strong you've grown."

Justus ran around the table to Longinus and put his little elbow on the table. It raised up so high he had no room for any leverage at all. Justus didn't know any better and continued on preparing for an arm wrestle. He pushed his fingers between his father's big hands. They barely poked through to lock on.

Priscilla smiled at the sight of them playing.

Longinus began to count, "One, two, three, go!"

Little Justus pushed his arm as hard as he could while Longinus resisted, and acted as though he just couldn't win. Finally little Justus pushed Longinus's massive arm to the table.

"I got stronger, see!"

Longinus lifted Justus high above his head.

"I see! You have grown like a bull!"

Priscilla watched on when suddenly she felt a sharp labor pain, then another and another. She looked at Longinus playing with Justus. She didn't want to interrupt their time together so she waited and refrained from outwardly showing any sign of growing pain. After a short while, the pains came closer and got so intense she could not hide the terribleness of it.

"Ahhh!" She screamed, "Longinus, go get Chloe. The baby is coming."

Longinus ran over to Priscilla. He hovered over her unsure what to do. She motioned for him to go get Chloe and he ran to the door. He heard Priscilla scream out again. He stopped and turned to go to her and she shouted at him again, this time in desperate agony.

"Go get Chloe. The baby is coming!"

"Justus, watch your mother. I'll be right back with Chloe. Justice stayed by his mother's side.

Longinus ran to the house of Chloe and banged on the door yelling her name repeatedly. Chloe came running to the door and took one look at the panicked Longinus and knew it was time for Priscilla to deliver.

Chloe instructed Longinus, "Go on, I will be right there."

Longinus took off back to Priscilla. Chloe grabbed a few things and ran out behind him. She got to the house and Priscilla was in hard labor. Justus was frightened by it all.

"Is mother dying?"

Chloe answered him, "No Justus. She will be fine soon."

Chloe motioned for Longinus to take Justus outside. He took Justus by the hand, "Come we wait outside now."

Longinus and Justus no sooner walked outside and Philip came running up. He fought to catch his breath to speak, "I saw you running from Chloe's house. Is Priscilla delivering?

"She is and with great pain. Justus and I will do better to wait outside."

"I will wait with you and Justus."

A short while passed and as Longinus, Justus and Philip were pacing, the sound of a newborn's cry was heard. Longinus ran to the house and leaped over the threshold entering the house.

Chloe handed Longinus a newly swaddled baby girl. He gingerly held her in his two hands, one around her head and the other under her small body. Tears of joy fell down his cheeks. He took a quick glance at Priscilla, then lovingly stared at the newborn. He spoke almost in a whisper, "She is pale but smiling."

Priscilla asked softly, "What name will you give her?"

He answered, "She shall be called Mary."

Priscilla smiled and answered, "I like that very much."

Justus walked into the room. Longinus called to him,

"Come, Justus see your sister, Mary."

THE SPEAR OF DESTINY II

Justus went to Longinus as he held out his baby sister and looked closely at her little hands. He smiled softly, "Her fingers are so tiny. Will they get big like mine?"

Longinus and Priscilla giggled at his words. Justus looked at them wondering what was so funny.

Priscilla came to his rescue, "My sweet Justus, she will grow strong and big like you."

She looked over and saw Philip standing back quietly.

"Come Philip, see little Mary."

Philip came close and gazed upon the newborn daughter.

"She is so beautiful. Such a miracle God has given you to have a child as this."

"Thank you Philip," said Mary, "We are truly blessed in many ways, your friendship is one."

"Priscilla, you are too kind. It is I that am blessed with the joy of your loving spirit."

Chloe looked outside and there were many people gathering. "My goodness, Mary, there are so many people coming to see your newborn. What will you have me do?"

Priscilla spoke, "Longinus will you take Mary to the doorway and show the people the child the Lord has blessed us with?"

Longinus nodded, still holding the baby tenderly, and went to the doorway. He proudly stood at the threshold.

"We have a daughter and her name is Mary."

The people joyfully gathered closer to get a better look at the newborn. Then, one by one, in an orderly manner, they walked pass Longinus and the baby to get a closer look and offered their best wishes. Some had brought gifts and passed them over to Chloe. There were lots of thankyous and the people were happy to be able to see the baby so soon.

Off in the distance stood a shadowy figure watching with less enthusiasm, it was the Sorcerer.

"My, my, so this is where the Enigma hides. Now aren't they all just so happy. I will fix that."

The Sorcerer spun around and disappeared.

A LAIR OF TROUBLE

The Sorcerer had returned to his Lair and was now busy throwing spices into a cauldron of hot, boiling brew.

"Ahah, this should do it," he sighed as he tossed in a pinch of orange powder.

He watched as the brew bubbled up then dissipated, leaving a thick film over the top.

"Now that the spear is hidden and only I know where it is, the enigma must meet his destiny's end."

He collected an assortment of spices from several jars and mixed them in a bowl. He threw them in the cauldron and watched as it violently frothed and foamed. He gazed into the cauldron and chanted a curse.

"Powers of darkness, rulers of sin, create a battle the followers can't win."

Immediately tormenting screams and cackles resonated loudly from within the cauldron. The brew settled and demons called out to him.

"Master, we have placed as you wish a new Caesar of Rome to do your bidding. Look at him."

The Sorcerer smiled at the image of an unpleasant balding man with a stern, almost sour looking face. The demons continue, "His name is Galba. We had to force him into power, it wasn't easy."

"Tell me, is he smart?"

"He's more of an arrogant self-serving aristocrat. He knows how to manipulate to meet his own agenda."

"Perfect."

The Sorcerer gazed into the cauldron and watched in real time what was taking place.

Galba was inside the palace with his advisor assessing the failures of Nero, and trying to plan a way to end Rome's headache of the stubborn Followers of the Way, and their protector, the Enigma.

Galba spoke, "The revolts are wide spread and Jerusalem continues to stand their armies against Rome."

His Advisor was eager to crush the Jews, "Just say the command and your Cohorts will crush the army of Jerusalem and kill all the troublesome zealots."

"Indeed," Galba was as ready as his advisor, "It is time to restore the power of Rome and put fear back into all who resist its' authority."

"Prefect, Sir, do you wish to call your Legate?"

"For what? To have him advise me? It was his advising Nero that created this chaos!"

"Perhaps to hold him responsible, Prefect?"

"I see. Yes. And do you suggest I replace him with another?"

"Indeed, Prefect. One who will do what Rome needs. "

"So be it. I shall replace him with someone who will crush this pesky resistance. Someone who knows how to slash all heads throughout the region of Jerusalem, Palestine, all the way to Cappadocia."

"Very wise decision, Prefect. Rome has enough to worry with the Parthians in Armenia. You must stop all rebellion of the Jews and their little war."

"I shall destroy all their secret places where they plot deceit and seek refuge."

"Prefect, the greatest rebel of all, the one they call the enigma, lives in Cappadocia. The one Nero could never defeat or capture. Get him, and they all go down."

"Then he shall be killed first."

"Prefect, might I add that he now has a wife and son."

"That should make it all the more easy."

The sorcerer looked up from the cauldron with a horrible evil grin and cackled.

"Ah-ha-ha, ha, ha,"

SURVIVAL INSTINCT

Longinus was at his house in the kitchen eating supper with his family. They were unexpectedly disrupted by someone banging hard on the door. Longinus looked surprised at Priscilla then got up to answer. A rebel stood there gasping for breath.

"What is it?" Asked Longinus.

"Rome is sending legions of soldiers to destroy all of Cappadocia's places of refuge. They are headed here."

"How far out are they?"

"A four week ride if they travel the fastest passage, six if they take the longer passage that has more villages." He stopped for his mouth was parched and dry.

Longinus grabbed his water cup and gave him a drink. The rebel drank and continued to speak.

"They are razing every village in their path, killing everyone sparing no lives. They seek to kill you and your family."

"I see," Longinus turned to Priscilla, "I must go to Khalid. Feed this good man."

Priscilla nodded and got up from her chair to fetch the man a bowl of food. Longinus put on his sword belt then left to find Khalid.

Khalid was putting provisions into his haversack from the storehouse. Longinus ran up to him. Khalid looked up and saw the fear in his eyes.

"Is there trouble?"

"Roman Cohorts are four weeks out. They come to kill the people and destroy our village."

Khalid was troubled, "We need more men to fight."

Longinus was looking at the task at hand more than mere wishes of having more men. "We must get every person and every supply of food and provisions into the underground passages beneath the chimney stacks. They will burn the village to the ground."

For the first time, Khalid had a look of panic. "There is no time to waste. I will send for help and alert the men."

He lifted his haversack over his shoulder and left in a hurry. Khalid ran directly to a Parthian who had great influence.

Khalid addressed him, "Who among you has great favor with your king?

The Parthian answered, "I have great favor."

"Will you go to your king and ask him to send his army to help us fight Romans in Cappadocia?"

The Parthian answered, "Our king is already at war with Rome for the throne of Armenia. To ask him to divide his army and send soldiers to Rome's Province of Cappadocia? I don't know if that is wise."

Khalid answered, "Wise or not, we must try,"

Another Parthian, Karim, overheard the conversation and stepped in front of Khalid.

"Our king has political motives and mutual hatred for Rome. He may oblige us. I will go."

"Go then," Khalid commanded, "There's no time to get provisions, here, take my haversack." He tossed the haversack full of provisions to Karim.

Karim grabbed it and nodded, then mounted his horse. He kicked him hard and galloped out of the village, headed to Parthia.

The first Parthian shook his head, "One less fighting man. You send him on a useless mission."

Khalid tried to control his anger at the remark but could not ignore it all together, "Mary, the elect one would say, we have not because we ask not. We shall ask."

The Parthian scoffed, "We shall see who is right in the end." He then left.

Khalid sighed and reached down to pat Vitali, something he did when he needed to calm down.

"Girl, we must always do what is laid on our heart to do." Vitali barked in agreement.

"We will leave the answer to God. Eh girl."

Vitali barked again.

"Come, we find Longinus." They left and returned to
 Find Longinus.

They searched for a while and finally found him standing by the hidden passageway in deep thought.

Longinus turned toward Khalid and watched him approach.

Khalid shared that he had sent a Parthian to the King for help. Longinus looked as eager about that as the Parthian who shared the same doubts.

"This is a serious matter and one we must prepare for as having the worst outcome, more than any of the other battles we have ever fought."

Khalid answered, "This I know full well."

"I must ask something great of you Khalid," Longinus took a deep breath, "Before I wed Priscilla, I had a dream of her in a coffin. She must leave this place. I want you to take her to Petra."

"You panic too fast. She will be safe in the underground passages. I need to stay and fight."

"The rebel told me they know I have a wife and children. I fear they seek to use them to make me surrender. Then kill us all."

Khalid's face grew pale in hearing that. Now he understood why Longinus's family must leave.

"Why Petra," asked Khalid.

"Petra is a hidden Bedouin fortress and a neutral ground whose trade on the spice route Rome values. And far enough away that Rome will not think to pursue any of us there."

"How do I find this place?"

"There are two ways in, but one way few make. It is through a narrow canyon. A man who once helped me and Mary was a merchant from there. He told us how to find this hidden way inside should we ever need to come."

"Who is this man?"

"His name is Arêtes. He will help us."

"How do we know he is still alive?"

"We don't. I only know God has laid it on my heart to send them there. So I obey," Answered Longinus.

Khalid nodded, "I will prepare provisions and some men to go with us. When should we go?"

"This very day. I will go and tell Priscilla."

Khalid nodded and went to prepare. Longinus went to talk to Priscilla.

Longinus hurried into his house and Priscilla was cleaning up the dishes from the table. He went to her with a serious look. Priscilla stopped what she was doing.

"What is it?" she asked concerned.

"Priscilla... my love, you must leave here with Justus and baby Mary. Khalid will take you to a safe place."

Firmly Priscilla answered him, "We will not leave here without you."

"Please Priscilla, this thing I ask you to do is hard enough. Please do not say such words."

Priscilla threw her arms around Longinus and embraced him hard. Tears streamed down her cheeks. Longinus was torn and held her tight. They clung to each other and little Justus came up to them.

"Mother, are we leaving papa?"

Longinus and Priscilla look down at Justus. Longinus bent down on his knee and took Justus by his shoulders looking him eye to eye in the face. "Son, there are evil men coming that do not know our ways. You must go with your mother and baby Mary to a place far off where you will be safe. I will come for you later. Know this."

"Papa no!" he cried.

"Justus, you are strong. I ask you to be stronger now. It is a hard thing. Son it must be."

Justus tried to fight back his tears, but they streamed down his cheeks as his lips quivered with sadness.

Priscilla mustered her strength and bent down on her knees in front of Justus. She gently stroked his head.

"Justus, we truly must go. Papa will come for us in time. It will be fine. I need you, my brave son to go and gather your things for the journey. Go now."

Justus wiped his tears and looked at his papa.

"I will be stronger," He hurried off into the other room and started to gather his things.

Priscilla looked at Longinus.

"I will gather our things. When must we leave?"

"At once. Khalid will take you to Petra."

"Petra? How do you know the people there will receive us?"

"Long ago, Mary and I met a man from Petra…Arêtes. He befriended us and told us of his city hidden in the mountains of Jordan. There is a way few know of through a sig. He told us how to find it if we ever needed refuge from Romans."

Priscilla questioned this. After all she was being sent out on a journey with a small child and a baby and needed reassuring it was wise.

"But that was long ago. Is he yet alive?"

Longinus answered, "I do not know. But he told us of his young son Arêtes II. If he is dead, his son will greet you, I am sure. Just tell him of Mary Magdalene. They spoke at length, privately and he favored her for she was blessed."

"I cannot bear to go without you. Please come with us instead of Khalid."

"Oh Priscilla, how I long to do that. If I go with you the Romans will pursue us all. Surely they will not stop until they kill you and our children. If I stay, they will only fight with me."

Priscilla looked at Longinus lovingly and heart broken.

"Surely, what you say is true. I have lived this before and my heart was broken. I must have faith that the day will come when we are all together again. I love you."

"Oh Priscilla, my heart beats only for you and our children. There is no way to describe my love for you."

Priscilla embraced Longinus. They stood together holding on tight for a long while. Each had a worried look and each were filled with sadness.

Longinus walked to the door and opened it. Priscilla followed him outside. He walked away from the house, then turned and ran back to Priscilla and embraced her tight.

One of the men called out to Longinus.

"I must go." Priscilla nodded and he left.

Watching from afar was Philip. He approached Priscilla.

"Oh Philip, I will miss you so."

"And I will you. Mary had said to watch over you and make certain no harm would come. But so be it, I grow old and unable to do as you need and your journey takes you away."

"Mother is always with me, she yet guides my heart."

"And your father too. I shall cling to the faith that God has sent you on this journey."

Priscilla took a deep breath and spoke, "This is a hard thing I must do, but, I shall be strong for Longinus and the children."

Priscilla left to gather her belongings.

A short while later...

Six strong men waited, mounted on their horses. They were dressed like Bedouin traders. A strong man was holding the reins to horses hitched to a wagon full of supplies for the journey.

Longinus stood looking up at Khalid on his horse.

"I leave them in your hands."

"They'll be safe. Between me and Vitali we'll have the heads of any who dare to touch'em."

Priscilla hurried over to the wagon holding baby Mary. Justus was running along at her side. They made their way to Khalid and the horses. Longinus gave one last hug to all of them, then picked up Justus and lifted him up to Khalid. Khalid situated him in the front of his saddle.

Longinus looked at his son and spoke to him like he was a man, "Justus, take care of Khalid. He needs a strong watchman as you!"

"I will Papa," He answered.

Khalid tried hard to keep his emotions intact and addressed Justus, "Just keep still in the saddle boy. Don't try to take charge or you ride in the wagon."

Justus gave a curious look.

Longinus touched his little leg and said, "Don't mind Khalid. He speaks the same to Vitali and you know who wins there."

Justus smiled.

Longinus's attention shifted to Priscilla. She was holding baby Mary and a man was helping her get into the wagon. She saw Longinus coming and had the man stop.

Longinus embraced her as she held tight to baby Mary. He reluctantly let go and leaned over giving baby Mary a kiss on her forehead.

He looked at Priscilla and touched her cheek softly, then kissed her on the lips. He said to her, "No matter what happens, know that I love you. You are the one who has given me great joy in my life and reason to live."

Priscilla answered, "And you, Longinus, have done the same for me."

The man helped Priscilla into the wagon. She looked out from the back of it at Longinus and said, "Please be safe. We will wait for you in Petra," Longinus nodded, then walked over to Khalid and looked at Justus one last time.

Khalid spoke, "We are ready."

Longinus answered, "Take them to safety and no matter what happens, give me your word you will guard them with your life."

Khalid shook his head, almost offended at having to be told again to guard them with his life for that is what he had always done.

"Just take care of the Romans and meet us in Petra," snapped Khalid.

Longinus smiled and nodded.

Khalid and the others began their ride out.

Priscilla held the baby tight and locked eyes with Longinus from the back of the wagon.

"Good by my loves," whispered Longinus under his breath.

Longinus stood watching until they were no longer in sight.

THE PARTHIAN KING - VOLOGESES

Two weeks had passed and Karim had made his way into the presence of King Vologeses in his court. He explained to the King the madness of Rome and was at the close of his plea to King Vologeses to send his Parthian army to assist Longinus in Cappadocia.

Karim pleaded, "The fires of Rome were set by Armenians, not by Longinus or any of his men who defend the innocent against endless slaughter. For years they have continued to slaughter all of the innocent in the villages and now come with a great army to kill everyone in the region."

The King answered, "I have word of the same."

Karim continued, "Stopping the Cohorts in Cappadocia will mean less Roman Soldiers for you to fight in Armenia."

King Vologeses respectfully responded, "I do not wish to be publically, nor secretly tied to this dispute. As you said, already I war with Rome for the throne of Armenia. But, if any in the Parthian army wish to fight another over a grievance that is a different matter."

He paused for a moment then added in a clever tone, "I care not who they fight on their own behalf."

After stating that, the King stood up, "Go now."

Karim sadly answered, "I understand, my King," He bowed and left.

King Vologeses watched him close as he left.

Two weeks later…

Longinus was busy overseeing the preparation of his village for Roman attack. They had stripped the city of any valuable items including food and water. Everything of value was taken to the underground passages that lie beneath the ground. No one knew how to enter them except Longinus, Khalid, and Philip. It had been a well-kept secret and not needed for a long while until this day. The houses were now virtually empty so that even if Roman soldiers set the village on fire, the losses would be less.

A watchman ran to Longinus and alerted him that Karim was returning from Parthia. Longinus stopped what he was doing and hurried to greet Karim as he rode in. Karim dismounted his horse and addressed Longinus.

"I regret my King does not want tied to this dispute. He wars enough in Armenia."

Longinus's heart sank but he hid it well.

"You did what you could."

"I wish I could have persuaded him."

"Perhaps my past hatred for Parthia is why his heart is cold toward our fate. Hate is not good. I know this now far too late in my life's destiny."

As Karim led his horse away, Longinus looked around at the village full of Parthians preparing for battle. He realized as though for the first time that without them all, he could have never saved so many, nor won so many battles. A sudden flood of remorse overcame him. He lifted his head toward the heavens and prayed,

"You gave me back my sight, but I have remained half blind. Today, my eyes are opened. All people are in your hands. I plead to you, forgive my blindness."

The next day, Longinus had just secured the last of the people in the underground passages. He was making sure all things were properly prepared when a man approached him.

"The boulders that block the passages have all been locked into place."

Longinus answered, "Good work. Take your positions."

The man left and another man came galloping in on horseback shouting, "The Romans are coming!" As he came closer he directed his shouts to Longinus, "They are less than four hours ride away!"

Longinus ran to his horse tied to a post in front of his house. He mounted and took one last look at his home and thought of Priscilla, Justus and baby Mary.

THE SPEAR OF DESTINY II

"There is no time for such thinking. It will get a strong man killed," He said under his breath.

He turned around and shouted to one of the men who was near, "The Romans approach. Sound the men to head to the outskirts. We must keep them from entering the village."

The man shouted back, "I go now!"

Longinus took a brisk ride through the village to make sure that the traps they had placed for the Romans were intact. Satisfied, he galloped his horse with great speed toward the outskirts to take his position with the band of men.

A short time later, Longinus arrived in the outskirts and addressed his lead man, Zikar.

"Are all things in place?"

Zikar, "Yes."

Longinus and Zikar waited silently and watched for the Romans to approach. In a short time the Roman cohort was spotted.

Longinus carefully waited for the right moment, then rode out so the Romans could see him. He carried a white flag with three blood red crosses and held it up high. It waved valiantly in the air as he galloped like the wind toward the cohort. When he reached a shouting distance between them, he stopped abruptly and reared his horse. There, he waited alone, holding the flag.

The Senior Centurion held up his hand. The Roman soldiers halted. Curious, the Senior Centurion awaited to see what Longinus would do.

Longinus stared out at the Roman Cohort then after a moment of silence and having all Roman eyes and ears upon him, he addressed them shouting deep and loud.

"On this day, destiny will decide who wins this war!"

He charged toward the Roman Cohort and shouted at the top of his lungs "DESTINY FAVOR ME!"

The Senior Centurion gave his command and the Roman horsemen charged forward toward Longinus. He gave another command and the infantry charged out behind them. Something that was never usually done.

The aggressive pursuit of Roman legions in such great number charging fiercely toward one lone man, was a sight to behold.

Longinus stampeded his horse toward the wall of Romans bravely charging to the left, then the right, crisscrossing back and forth strategically along the way, then suddenly without any warning Longinus turned his horse and headed back in the direction from which he came, riding to the left and the right, crisscrossing in the same manner.

He appeared to the Romans as one who had changed his mind about marching into death and decided to retreat.

The Roman horsemen did not falter, they continued to charge after Longinus and were almost at his heels gaining on him when Longinus's horse made an amazing leap in the air hurling over the ground as though it was crossing a river. All at once the charging Romans suddenly fell one by one into unseen pits that had been camouflaged by sticks and dried grass.

Roman horsemen tried in vain to halt and turn their horses but they could not. They fell into the pits. The few horsemen who were able to halt, were left only to be trampled from the stampede of horsemen behind them charging forward falling into the pits.

The charging foot soldiers suddenly began falling into pits throughout the battle field in the same places Longinus had strategically avoided by riding to the left and the right. The screams of death echoed throughout the battle field when suddenly, the sky was blackened with arrows coming from over the canyon, raining down like locusts, onto the Roman archers whose bows were drawn. The archers shielded themselves but a great number were struck and fell to the ground.

The band of men rode out like a storm from the canyon walls. The Romans charge forward at the men bellowing out ear piercing shouts as their swords clanged in great battle. The remaining Roman archers shot their arrows and the sky blackened again, this time falling on the band of men.

Suddenly, on the horizon, appeared another Roman Cohort. Their horsemen rode in strong. Longinus saw them coming and with his sword readied, kicked his horse, and galloped with great speed to meet the Cohort head on in battle.

The situation which had looked so promising now appeared to be one that was impossible for victory. There was no way Longinus's men could stay off the second Roman Cohort.

In spite of all the odds, Longinus and his men continued to battle valiantly. Retreating was not an option.

Then out of nowhere the ominous roar of approaching horsemen was heard again. The ground trembled from the vibration of thundering hooves. Longinus peered out in the distance and saw a cloud of dust stirring above the canyon.

He thought another Roman Cohort was descending on the battle field. Feeling this was his day to die, he shouted at the top of his lungs, "Lord, receive my soul!"

He battled on with all his might slashing his sword against a Roman horseman. As the Roman fell from his saddle, Longinus was blinded by a piercing light coming from over the horizon.

None of the soldiers could see to fight as the light permeated throughout the battlefield. While they all fumbled about shielding their eyes, a massive army of ornately decorated horses and their riders appeared from out of the canyon walls and swiftly encircled the battlefield.

Meanwhile, a greater number of horsemen ornately decorated the same as those that rode out from the canyon, stood on the horizon holding their shields to the sun. The golden orb shimmered mercilessly onto the battlefield blasting out like the glory of God, blinding every eye that looked toward it. All shielded their eyes from the burning, illuminating light.

Longinus squinted to see who these were and saw it was the Royal Parthian army of King Vologeses. They continued to charge from over the horizon in rows so deep, no one could guess the number of them.

Longinus stood still and spoke in awe, "Parthians! My Lord, has moved the hearts of men to grant us great favor!"

At that, Longinus swung his sword with a burst of renewed strength at a Roman aggressor, striking him down.

The same newfound energy surged through the veins of the entire band of men as they cheered explosively at the arrival of the Parthians!

The Parthians rode steady in their saddles with no hands shooting arrows that blackened the sky. Longinus thrust his horse's side with his heels and the horse shot forward like a rocket away from the path of the arrows.

Once out of the path of flying arrows, Longinus reared up his horse, waving his sword in the air as the soaring arrows pummeled down upon the Roman cohort. He looked up to the heavens and shouted.

"Victory is yours!"

He held out his sword and charged deep into the battle, slaying all who cast their sword at him. The Parthians mercilessly sliced the Romans, sending heads and body parts flying through the air. The battle raged on. Finally the last of the remaining Romans retreated in defeat.

Longinus swiftly rode his horse up to the decorated Parthian who led the charge.

He firmly, but humbly spoke to him, "I am in the debt of Parthia."

The Parthian leader answered, "King Vologeses has seen us as one."

Longinus declared to him, "When you return to King Vologeses, tell him that Longinus has said, indeed, this day we are one."

THROUGH THE SIG

After a long journey, Khalid, Priscilla, her children and their entourage had finally entered the passageway through the narrow canyon into Petra.

Khalid directed the men, "This is where we must enter."

The gorge entrance was very difficult to judge from the ground, all of it looked the same.

"The directions Longinus gave me points this way. What say you Vitali?"

Vitali barked and Khalid smiled, "She says it feels right. We go."

They proceeded through the narrow gorge, and after a long while Priscilla looked out from the front of the wagon. She was amazed at the most breath taking view of an exotic, glistening architecture.

Priscilla was excited and shouted, "Justus! Look and see where your father has sent us too!"

Justus looked out and stared in awe. Stunned, he watched in a state of wonder. A radiant golden, rose red, structure as heavenly to Justus as if the angels had designed it themselves, stood out proudly through a narrow opening in the sig. The darkened shadowy sides of the gorge contrasting against the sun kissed architectural wonder was magical to behold.

Khalid shouted proudly, "Priscilla get ready, we are almost through this sig."

Priscilla tied back the flap on the wagon fully opening the view so Justus could see everything. She looked over at Khalid riding beside them on his horse.

"This is truly a wonder. Longinus sent us here wisely."

They continued to travel through the sig and entered into Petra. The buildings were immense and ornate in design, majestically carved into the rock of the colorful sandstone mountains. They continued a ways and stopped in front of an enormous, monumental building.

Priscilla hollered to Khalid from the wagon, " We must ask for the son of Arêtes!

Justus looked out at the building and shouted, "Mother look! We are like ants to the people who go through these doors."

She answered him, "Justus there is a history here you cannot comprehend. Indeed, we are as ants."

As they proceeded into Petra, a man approached them. Khalid addressed him, "We seek a man. Arêtes."

The man asked, "Why do you seek him?"

"For safety and refuge. By promise to Mary Magdalene."

"Then I show you. Follow me."

Khalid followed the man through the streets as he led the way. He brought them to an ornate building carved in the rock.

"Arêtes son lives here. He is Arêtes II. Go and call on him."

Khalid smiled and said, "Thank you, good man."

The man nodded, then turned and left. Khalid dismounted and helped Priscilla and baby Mary out from the wagon. Justus hopped down behind them.

Khalid announced, "Come, we find this man named Arêtes II."

ALL ARE ONE

Longinus and his men returned to the village victoriously from battle. He was relieved that the Romans never entered their village and it was spared from being destroyed. He was still in awe at the manner the Lord had moved the heart of his self-perceived arch enemy, the Parthian King Vologeses, to send his mighty royal army to save them from the hands of the Romans.

Longinus, though physically exhausted was energized in spirit. "Zikar, go and tell the men to alert our people hidden in the underground passages throughout the village that the Lord has given us a great victory this day."

Zikar nodded and went to do as he was told.

Longinus added, "Caution them to stay underground until we know it is safe." Zikar motioned with his hand that he would do so.

Longinus went to one of the underground passages. He made his way through a narrowing rocky tunnel and came to a boulder blocking the passage. He took a flask of water and poured it out next to the boulder. He watched as it slowly seeped under it.

A man in the passage saw the water and pulled a lever and the boulder slid to the side, opening the passage.

Longinus entered. Once he was inside, the man pulled a lever and the boulder rolled back in place blocking the opening.

Longinus asked, "Where is Philip?"

"Come," answered the man, "He is over this way."

Longinus followed him through the passageway to a group of people. Philip was among them.

Longinus eagerly told them of the victory. The people cheered, praising God and thanking Longinus. He smiled and nodded and motioned for Philip to follow him. Philip followed him to a secluded part of the underground passage.

"I must speak with you," Said Longinus. Philip nodded and listened attentively. "Today, a cohort of Romans came at us. They fell in our traps. As we went forth in battle another Roman cohort came. We were outnumbered. Then over the horizon and through the canyon came an army of Parthians so great I cannot tell you the number of them who came to our defense giving us great victory. Without the Parthians, we would have been defeated."

Philip spoke, "So you wonder at why Parthians came to battle beside you?"

"I believe God sent them. I am ashamed of my blindness to their own persecution by Romans. And how I scoffed at Khalid for sending a man to ask such favor."

"Longinus, in God's Kingdom there is no Parthian, no Roman, no Jew. All are one in his eyes."

"The Parthian General said, in Vologeses eyes we are one. I do not understand these things."

Philip thought a moment then answered, "No one is without a wrong. God looks at the heart of each. Not the outside actions. All life is precious to him."

"What of those who kill the innocent?"

Philip asked, "Did you not ever kill an innocent because you were ordered to do so as your Roman soldier duty?"

"That was allegiance to Rome. I was a Centurion."

"God knows this. He also knows each innocent that was killed according to a Roman soldier's duty. He knows each who has been killed by any man's hand."

Longinus hung his head down.

Philip continued, "Were not the Romans today doing their Roman duty?"

"Rome who I once served sought to kill us. The Parthians who I hated came to help us. This is what I am trying to make sense of."

"We are all the same in God's eyes. It is man that makes the wars. This is the way of prince of the world. Jesus knew this and told us we are in the world but not of the world and they would even kill us thinking they do God a favor."

Longinus answered, "And that is what they think!"

"Sadly, you are right."

Longinus declared, "I must go to Priscilla. You and the people must stay in the passages until the men tell you it is safe."

Philip cautioned, "Be careful."

Longinus nodded and left through the passage.

Arêtes II

Back in Petra, Khalid and Priscilla have finally met Arêtes II. They were invited inside and given food and drink. They sat together at the table with him, and talked of many things, including a past that Priscilla had many unanswered questions about.

Justus sat next to his mother quietly, listening to every word that was spoken as if a great story were being read to him. Baby Mary was cradled safely in Priscilla's arms and Khalid was still eating.

Arêtes II, "My father would always say Mary is of God. I remember when he welcomed your people. You were so young."

"I was no older than Justus. It is all hard to remember. But this place I could never forget. No one ever told me its' name."

Arêtes II, "That was for your protection."

"When they brought me here, my heart was broken and I longed for my mother and father. I did not know what was happening then."

Arêtes II comforted her, "Once again, you shall be safe here."

Khalid clumsily added, "We wait for Longinus. When he comes Vitali and I will decide where to go. For now I stay and protect Priscilla, Justus and Mary."

Arêtes II nodded.

Khalid sighed and pushed his empty plate forward, "I'm getting too old to fight. Vitali is strong and has not aged, but she too is tired of war."

Arêtes II stood up, "Come. I will show you where you may stay,"

They got up and followed Arêtes II.

WARNING DREAMS

Longinus was well on his journey to reach Petra and had come as far as Syria. He had not eaten food, nor rested since the battle with Rome. His body was running on sheer adrenaline, coupled with passion to see Priscilla and his children. But now, exhaustion and hunger had taken over and he knew it was time to stop and make camp. And so he did.

Some time later:…

Longinus had just finished eating and was now making up his bed roll. He reached over and poked the fire to make sure the embers would smolder. He lay down and looked up at the stars thinking of Priscilla until he fell asleep and began to dream.

In his dream, Priscilla was standing in Petra holding out his spear crossways in the palms of her hands. Longinus went to her and took the spear.

As soon as he lifted if from her palms, an evil dark figure appeared.

Khalid approached and the dark figure waved his hand at him and he disappeared.

A lion approached and Priscilla walked over to the lion's side. They both faded away.

Then the dark figure gave a sinister grin and started to advance his way toward Longinus. The dream abruptly ended.

Longinus awakened trembling.

"It is but a dream," He said out loud to himself. He looked up in the night sky and a shooting star sailed across and fell from sight. He called out as though he were talking to someone standing in front of him, "What are you telling me?"

He lay back down and watched the night sky. His mind wondered about the dream and the shooting star, but he was too exhausted to think and fell back to sleep.

That same night, at the same hour in Petra, Priscilla was sleeping and she too had a dream.

In her dream she saw Justus looking at a stone statue of a man. Longinus came and looked at the statue. Suddenly an angel appeared. A boulder next to the statue vibrated and rolled away exposing an open gaping hole. Longinus looked at the hole and climbed into it. He came back out of the hole holding the spear. Priscilla saw Khalid coming with Vitali at his side. Khalid slowly faded away. Her children appeared. Justus and little Mary, they are now much older. She watched as they walked away with Longinus. The dream ended.

Priscilla woke up frightened and wondered of the dream. An angel appeared to her.

"Do not be frightened. The past, present and future must come together within Longinus for him to fulfill his destiny. Until he sees all time is happening at the same time as one circle in a part of a fleeting moment, he shall remain blind to understanding his purpose."

Priscilla asked the angel, "What is it that I must do?"

The angel answered, "Longinus has been granted time to rest from war and you have been granted time to be with him and teach him. When this rest comes to the close of its' allotted time, you will know it. At that time you must tell Longinus of your true past so he can complete his destiny."

Priscilla watched as the angel lifted up and faded away as he ascended. She said a prayer of thanks, then lay back down and closed her eyes to sleep.

GALBA'S DEFEAT IS JERUSALEM'S WOE

Back in Rome, Galba had received the report that King Vologeses army interceded in his battle plans against the Enigma and the destruction of his village. He was more frustrated at the loss of his much wanted victory than he was of the loss of over his cohorts of Roman soldiers.

Galba addressed the Senior Centurion, "So Vologeses now guards Cappadocia."

The Senior Centurion answered, "Yes, Prefect. He guards with so great an army they cannot be numbered."

Galba hated losing, but was not a fool. He would not go up against Vologeses after hearing such a report. But, any victory is a victory and he needed one now before any of the senate started to criticize his leadership.

"Then we turn our attention to Jerusalem and throughout all of Palestine."

Senior Centurion, "Yes, Prefect, Sir."

"I trust you can give me a victory quickly to offset your bad report in Cappadocia."

"Yes Prefect, Sir."

Galba peered at him with distain, "Are you certain?"

"Yes Prefect, Sir."

"One more thing," Galba paused for a moment, "I trust you shall keep the numbers of the dead Roman Soldiers at a minimum range in your report to the Senate."

The Senior Centurion hesitated, then he answered, "Yes, Prefect, Sir."

"And I trust you shall add in your report that the village was burned and the followers killed."

The Senior Centurion grew pale, "Prefect, Sir…"

Galba interrupted, "I trust you shall do as I ask? Or would you rather be stripped of your rank? If not by me, by the Senate for certain if you don't do as I say. Do you understand?"

The Senior Centurion answered quickly, "Yes, Prefect, Sir."

Galba was satisfied with that and ordered, "You have your orders. Go now and don't come back without a victory."

The Senior Centurion bowed and left.

In the shadows of the Palace, a dark figure lurked. He had overheard the entire account and was more angry than Galba at the report.

The dark figure mumbled under his breath, "So the enigma wins again. I shall find another way to stop him."

The dark figure stepped out from the shadows, it was the Sorcerer. He spun around and disappeared.

THE REUNION

After much travel, Longinus had finally reached the narrow gorge that led into the rose red city of Petra. His heart raced as he rode his horse through the passage eager to reach the mystical city that was home to ornate carved structures. For it was there that his wife and children whom he longed to see, were safely tucked away in the bosom of the colorful basin between the majestic sandstone mountains.

He galloped along swiftly in spite of all of the protruding cliffs, and narrowed, twisting turns and only slowed as he came upon the most breathtaking view of 'Al Khazneh', the ancient Treasury peeking proudly through the narrowing of the sig. Taking it in, his heart filled with joy knowing Priscilla was somewhere on the other side.

He kicked his horse and rode fast through the sig and into the city. He slowed his horse to a trot and stopped to talk to a well-dressed man buying wares.

"A group of people with a wagon were to come here. Did they arrive?

"The man asked, "Who are you that wish to know this?"

"I am Longinus."

The man motioned to Longinus and said, "Come with me."

Longinus dismounted his horse and walked with the man, leading his horse behind him. The man took him deep into the city. He stopped and pointed over to a section of houses built up in the cliffs of the rock.

"Start at the steps carved in the path and follow it up. You will go down a narrow opening carved between the mountains. From there, follow up the second set of winding steps in the rock. That will lead you to the housing quarters. There you will find them. The path is not made to take a horse, tie him to the post."

Longinus thanked the man and proceeded to do as he was told. As he tied his horse he eyed a little boy and an older youth looking at a stone statue. He looked closely and it was Justus. He ran to him and shouted, "JUSTUS!"

The little boy turned and his eyes widened and he smiled from ear to ear, he ran toward Longinus, and leaped into his arms, shouting, "PAPA! PAPA!"

Longinus lifted Justus up and gave him a long, hard embrace. He went around in a circle then put him back down on the ground. "Where is your mother?" he asked, at the same time Longinus caught a glimpse of the statue. He walked toward it to get a closer look at the face. It looked like Armond.

"Mother is at the house in the rock. This is my friend Jafar. He is showing me many new things."

Longinus still staring at the statue told Justus, "Have Jafar take you to your mother and tell her I am here."

Justus and Jafar ran to tell his mother that Papa was here.

Longinus touched the statue. Suddenly the ground vibrated. An angel appeared and the stone rolled away exposing a hole. Longinus could not see the angel for the angel shut his eyes from seeing him.

Longinus walked over and peered inside the hole. He saw a bright light shining through cracks between a layer of scattered rocks. Curious he jumped down inside the hole. He stood over the shining beam and dug through the rock and stone. He felt something hard beneath a cloth. He pulled it up and unwrapped the cloth. It was the head of his spear. He put it inside his shirt and hurried out from the hole.

Once out of the hole he pulled the spear from inside his shirt and marveled at how it could have gotten in the hole under the boulder. His mind was thinking of all manner of things when Priscilla and Justus came running toward him.

"See," yelled Justus, "It is Papa!"

Priscilla's smile turned into a gasp when she saw the statue of Armond and Longinus holding the spear tip. Longinus dropped the spear and grabbed Priscilla. He held her tight. Justus picked up the spear head and looked at it curiously.

Priscilla and Longinus kissed. Then Priscilla asked, "How did you find the spear head?"

"Justus was looking at the statue. I saw that it looked like Armond and touched it. The boulder moved uncovering this hole. I looked and saw the tip of the spear and took it from the hole."

"Longinus, I saw this all in a dream."

Suddenly Longinus remembered his own dream.

"I too, had a dream. In it you gave me the spear," Longinus became fearful as he thought of his dream.

Priscilla recognized that look Longinus got when he was about to go into a state of frustrating confusion. She consoled him, "Do not fear. Longinus for when I awoke an angel came to me and said you would be granted a time to rest from war. Things must take place for you to follow your destiny."

Longinus looked at Justus fiddling with the spear head. He reached over and took the spear head from him.

"I must mount this spear to a strong shaft."

Priscilla took Longinus by the arm, "Come, I will show you where we stay. You must be hungry,"

A little while later, they were all gathered around the table eating and listening to Longinus tell of the great battle against the Romans and the triumphant entry of the army of King Vologeses. There was no way he could embellish such an event, in fact his words fell short of ever fully describing the magnificence of such divine intervention that he rightfully contributed to a power from above.

When Longinus had finished his telling of all that took place, Khalid smiled and said, "Then my sending the Parthian to his king helped? Yes?"

"Without his help, Khalid, we would have suffered a miserable loss, and I would not be here now."

Khalid was more than satisfied with hearing those words. He looked down at Vitali, "Girl, this old bounty hunter still has instinct." Vitali barked.

Longinus smiled, "That's why I sent you to guard Priscilla."

Khalid blushed and changed the subject, "I know a man who can mount your spear. I will show you, but first, you must go and meet Arêtes II."

A short time later...

Khalid had introduced Longinus to Arêtes II and Longinus told him of the Roman battle and King Vologeses army bringing them to victory.

"It is wise to stay here until the unrest settles," offered Arêtes II, "Romans will not seek you here."

But, Longinus was not afraid of war and answered, "There are battles that must be fought to save the Followers of the Way."

"Others will fight the good fight," Stated Arêtes II, "It is wise now for you to consider what is best to protect your family."

Longinus thought for a moment, "Perhaps you are right."

"So you will stay?" inquired Arêtes II.

Longinus answered, "For now."

Arêtes smiled and said, "When the time is come to go you will know it. Now is not that time."

Longinus nodded, "Rome lives to war. There will always be battles, but not always family."

They got up to leave and Khalid said to Longinus, "Now I take you to the man who can mount your spear."

Longinus responded, "There is plenty of time for that. Since I stay a while, there is no hurry."

Khalid shrugged his shoulders and looked down at Vitali, "He changes his mind always."

Vitali barked.

12 YEARS LATER, THE DEATH NOTICE

12 years have passed and the year is now 81 AD. As though under a curse, Rome has had a succession of evil "wanna be" failed Caesars and all of them sought to kill the Followers as well as anyone who got in their way.

In less than a year, Galba was slain in the streets by guardsmen on horseback at the will of an ambitious senator named Otho who was then proclaimed Caesar of Rome.

In a few short months, another scoundrel named Vitellius, with selfish ambitions, battled Otho's soldiers resulting in the so-called suicide of Otho and Vitellius seizing the throne by military coupe. More of a tyrant than Nero, he executed everyone he believed had wronged him, creating such a bloodbath that it led, within a few short months, to the rise of Flavius Vespian.

Vespian led his troops to overtake Vitellius, pulling him from his hiding place in the palace and took him to the Forum where the crowds ridiculed him while a man stabbed him to death. Vespian re-established some sense of order in Rome and ruled for ten years.

Vespian was succeeded by his son Titus whose short reign led Rome through the eruption of Mount Vesuvius, followed by another great fire that burned Rome, and an epidemic of disease that killed masses of people, ending in his own death by fever, although some said it was by the hand of his younger brother Domitian. Either way, his death led to the rise of his thirty year-old brother, Domitian whose first rule of order was to set forth a wave of cruel persecution against the Followers.

Domitian's hatred was far reaching and extended to the death of Roman senators; some for vengeance and some to confiscate their wealthy estates. But, the most chilling decree of all was his command that all the lineage of David be put to death.

Meanwhile, back in Petra, Longinus had been blessed with 12 years of actually being a husband and a father. Their lives had been peace filled and full of happiness. Justus was now 15 years old and had grown into a handsome young man, with his mother's eyes and his father's physic. Mary was now 12 and blossoming into a beautiful young woman resembling Priscilla in her mannerisms and helpfulness. But her facial features and smile was that of her grandmother Mary.

When the news of Domitian's evil decree came to Longinus, he was having a typical day being a father to his son while Priscilla was busy preparing the family meal.

Longinus was having fun showing Justus how to win a battle in a mock fight with wooden swords bantering back and forth in Priscilla's way as she tried to place loaves on the fire without getting poked.

Justus was just as serious at beating his father in a sport now as he was when he was a small child and sullied his wooden sword relentlessly to win. The two of them bantered about the small room and accidently knocked over an urn of water. Little Mary quickly picked up the pitcher and took a rag to sop it up.

Priscilla gave Longinus a stern look, "What am I to do with you two? Go now, take your practice outside."

Longinus jerked his head at Justus, motioning for him to follow outside. They both hurried out before Priscilla could say another word.

They continued to banter their swords back and forth.

Khalid approached and walked toward them with Vitali at his side. Once a giant of a man standing 6 foot 7 with shoulders almost as broad, Khalid has now aged and walked a bit bent and stiff. His skin has grown dry and full of scratchy lines around his eyes, and forehead. His voice is still deep, but, no longer resounding as thunder. It had grown breathy, and raspy. Whereas, Vitali had not aged a bit.

"When you are done, I need to speak with you."

Longinus stopped and handed Justus his wooden sword, "Enough for now." Justus took the sword and left.

Khalid paced back and forth as though searching for the words to say what was on his mind. Longinus was used to this behavior in Khalid, and waited patiently for him to find his words.

"This is a hard thing," he said with a hoarse, honeyed sound, he quickly cleared his throat to speak deeper, "Word has come that Rome is massacring the followers by the hundreds and spares no one. They are out to kill all that belong to the lineage of David in all the provinces."

"It is time to mount my spear to a strong shaft."

Khalid responded, "I am too old to fight. You have family. Let others fight with Rome."

"Khalid, it was hard not to fight when I heard of them burning scrolls, and parchments along with followers, and destroying the temple, killing all the Jews and followers throughout the region. All these horrid things tore at my heart. I can no longer shut my eyes to this."

Khalid's eyes were saddened, "I never beg, but I do now. You must put family first."

"My family will understand."

Khalid shook his head and closed his eyes.

"Wait here," Longinus shot off toward the house.

Priscilla looked over and watched Longinus hastily take his spear from its resting place, then briskly leave without saying a word. She knew the time had come and whispered softly under her breath, "I must tell him of my past."

As Khalid led Longinus to the blacksmith Longinus kept glancing at him. He noted how he labored in his walk to keep up and breathed hard, even wheezing a few times. This was not the man he once knew. It was finally soaking in that Khalid had grown old. He wondered how he had not noticed this before now.

"Why is it that when one grows old, it is a thing that can't be seen until there is a trouble?"

Khalid gave Longinus an odd look.

"Like Mary. I never saw her as old until the night she could not get up without grabbing the edge of the wall and tried hard to hide her pain."

Longinus face turned sad.

"You don't see age coming," Answered Khalid, "One day it just happens."

Longinus's mind was filled thoughts of his last time with Mary and kept going back further and further until he thought of things he hated to think about.

"I am younger now than I was the day I....I"

"Why are you tormenting me with this talk?" Gruffed Khalid.

"It is how I do."

"Yea, well it's time ya learn not to do so much of it. Lest not around me. Right Vitali?"

Vitali barked.

"I can't do such things," sighed Longinus.

Khalid huffed, "But you can slow down a bit and give an old bounty hunter time to catch his breath."

Longinus chuckled and walked a bit slower.

In a little while they came to the place of the blacksmith and was greeted by a short man with a proud smile.

"I'm Kareem, what can I do for you?"

Longinus unwrapped the spearhead from the cloth and held it out.

"I need this mounted on the strongest shaft you can make."

The blacksmith took the spear head and examined it.

"I can do wood, but this deserves a fine metal. One of light weight."

"Metal?"

"I can forge a metal lighter than wood and stronger than any iron. I can even clean up the head and make it shine."

"The spear shines enough. Do not touch it with even a cloth. Just mount it on the strongest wood."

The blacksmith rolled his eyes, "Come back tomorrow. It will be ready."

THE KNOWING

After a long day, Longinus and Priscilla had gone to bed. Priscilla softly laid her head on Longinus's chest. He cradled his arm around her.

Struggling with the right time to speak, Priscilla realized there would be no perfect time, nor any perfect setting. It was a thing she just needed to do and get it over with.

"There is something I must tell you."

"You sound serious. What is it?"

Priscilla took a deep breath and began to tell him of her past. "Long ago when I was a little child I was fast asleep and my mother came running into the house in the night and woke up everyone in the house. She grabbed up my brother, who was just a baby and told my Aunt to help her grab things we would need for a journey. I watched as they ran and grabbed this and that.

"I remember my Aunt picking me up and we all ran from the house. It all happened so very fast. My mother ran to a house and knocked hard on the door. A man answered and mother told him they had arrested her master. She pleaded with them to watch over us while she went to see what they planned to do with him. They agreed.

"My Aunt let me down, and I stood there frightened. I had never seen mother so scared. I watched my mother run fast away, until they took me from the doorpost and shut the door tight.

"I worried and waited for mother to come back. She did not return until the next night. When she came she kissed me and hugged me tight. She told me I had to be very brave and stay with my Aunt and the people for a little while. She kissed me good bye and I clung to her side. She hugged me and told me to be strong and help take care of the baby. She gave him a kiss and tears rolled down her cheeks. She quickly wiped them away. I cried hard when she left, I was so frightened.

"Some days went by, I don't remember how many, a week I think. And my Aunt took me and my brother with other people to a place far away. That is what they called it. They never mentioned the place by name. We were there for a long time that felt like an eternity. They kept telling me mother was fine and would come for me soon. It was almost a year and she still never came.

"Finally my uncle came and took me, my brother, my aunt and others on a long journey to a port where we got on a boat. We sailed to the South of Gaul and mother was standing on the shore waiting for us. My heart was filled with joy and sadness at the same time when she told me that father was no longer with us in the flesh but was alive in our hearts.

"I stayed in the South of Gaul until I agreed to help the Followers of the Way in Cappadocia."

Longinus was mournful for Priscilla's tragedy and at a loss for words. He embraced her heavily, perhaps more to comfort himself than her.

"I did not know you had such heartbreak."

Priscilla took a deep breath and said, "My mother was Mary Magdalene."

Longinus lifted straight up in bed and exclaimed, "WHAT?!"

Priscilla repeated herself, "My mother was Mary Magdalene."

Longinus embraced Priscilla, as tears ran down his cheeks. After a while, he composed himself and loosed his embrace. He gently took Priscilla by the shoulders and looked directly into her loving eyes.

"Our children… Mary is their grandmother?"

She softly answered, "Yes."

"She never spoke of any of this. What happened to your father?"

"That does not matter. I have said enough. It is a lot for you to bear."

Longinus sat frozen trying to process all he was told. He vacillated between shock and puzzlement.

There was much more to tell Longinus, but Mary did not know how much more he could bear, for he always acted out impulsively and thought his actions through long afterwards. She reasoned within her heart and knew that she must tell the most important part of the message now. Right now.

"Khalid told me of Rome's mandate to kill all of the line of David, Longinus, I tell you the truth this very day, I and our children are of that line."

"How? Mary spoke never of such a thing?"

"She was in great danger and just like all the Followers of the Way, they sought to kill her. She spoke nothing of herself, or her family to protect us all."

"I know. I protected her always. I rescued her and others from the prisons. I had thought it was because she was a follower."

"It was. But more than that she had great influence, she was the Magdalene of the tribe of Benjamin."

Longinus showed his confusion so Priscilla knew she must explain it further and make it simpler for him to understand.

"My mother was called Mary of Magdalene for the reason that she was the chief female heir to the tribe of Benjamin and Heir to the line of David. She was what my people called the Magdalene of the tribe of Benjamin."

"She told me none of this, she told me she hailed from the fishing village, Magdalene."

"The village was named after the chief tribe of Benjamin. In my language of Hebrew, the word pillar means Magdal. It stands for the one who holds authority. The name Magdalene means the great pillar female one. She was the great supreme woman of her tribe of Benjamin."

Longinus was piecing it all together, "And now the Romans seek to kill you and our children. My destiny is becoming more clear. The past is now the present."

Priscilla immediately remembered her dream and the angel who told her that Longinus must first find his past, present, and future in order to fulfill his destiny. She now understood its' meaning. But would he? She wondered if she should tell him of the angel's words? No, she thought, the angel said he must discover it for himself. Instead, she thought to encourage him, for it was the future that he was yet to discover.

Priscilla spoke assuredly, "Romans can never destroy the throne of David. Evil men seek to do such things, but evil will never prevail."

"Then I must not leave you. I must stay here and guard the line of David."

THE SORCERERS REVENGE

The following morning Longinus was eager to set out to the Blacksmith to get his spear. His mind was full of thoughts and wonderment of how God had given him such an important purpose. He had never imagined that he was guarding a royal lineage, and it was incomprehensible for him to even begin to understand how or why he had been allowed to marry into it. Was this always his destiny? He did not know what to believe or not believe concerning himself in the entire plan god had for him. Could this be why he does not age and lives on and on? He was confused at all of it. None of it made sense, and it all sounded like a Greek fairy tale to him.

Meanwhile, the blacksmith was looking at the spear head that Longinus dropped off. He had just finished going through his shafts, testing them all before he selected the strongest one. He was now ready to mount the blade and peered at it strangely as he rolled if over in his hands. He thought it a dull and dirty thing not worth mounting on such a strong shaft. But that was just his opinion.

He took up a cloth and dared to wipe it clean, even though Longinus had told him not to do so.

He began to rub it clean and sparks flew out from it burning his hand, he dropped it fast and stuck his hand in a barrel of water.

He pulled his hand out of the water to check how badly it was burned and there was no mark on it at all. It looked as though nothing had happened!

"Well, I'll be." "He wondered at how that happened, but didn't try to clean it again. He proceeded to make a strong fit and went about his process of mounting.

Back at the Sorcerers Lair...

At the exact same time the sparks flew out from the spear, the Sorcerer felt a disturbance. He was busy going through his spices and suddenly stopped what he was doing. He looked up, out and around. He sniffed the air and smelled a burning. He ran to his sphere and looked into it. The blacksmith in Petra appeared. He was finishing the mounting of the spearhead to a strong shaft.

"This cannot be?" He queried, "How?"

He curiously continued to watch and saw Longinus enter the Blacksmith's shop. He watched as Longinus tested it out and paid the blacksmith.

"Now just what is *HE* doing in Petra?"

The Sorcerer spun around and disappeared.

In an instant he reappeared in Petra in front of the stone statue of Armond. He looked around and saw the boulder was rolled away. He leaned over and looked into the gaping hole then over at the statue. He sneered at it and said, "Even in stone you cannot do what you promise,"

The Sorcerer waved his hand and the statue crumbled into dust. He turned around and taunted, "Now to find Longinus."

The Sorcerer lurked about Petra and found nothing unusual going on. He sniffed the air and turned. His eyes went right to Vitali. Khalid was by his side. "I thought I smelled that damn dog," He hurried over to the shadows of the rock and stood quietly observing them.

"Well, well, now just what are they doing here?"

The Sorcerer walked out from the shadows up to Khalid and purposely startled him. He laughed and mockingly jeered at him,

"I see mortality always pays its' toll on those borrowing from its' time! Does it hurt now to run? To bend?"

Khalid angrily shouted, "What do you want?!"

"My, my, Vitali looks the same. What do you feed her?"

Vitali growled and showed her teeth.

Fearing for Vitali, Khalid shouted, "Go Vitali – get Longinus!" Vitali bolted away like lightning.

The Sorcerer smiled, "Well now, I couldn't have asked you to do any better."

Khalid realized he was just tricked. He pulled his dagger and hurled it at the Sorcerer. The Sorcerer raised his hand and the dagger froze in mid-air. In slow motion the dagger turned. It hung for a moment floating, then with lightning speed the dagger hurled back at Khalid piercing through his heart. Khalid grabbed hold of the dagger with both hands and fell to his knees. The Sorcerer walked over grinning. Khalid looked up at the Sorcerer eye to eye.

"You do not kill me, you just send me to eternal life faster than time would have taken me."

The Sorcerer cringed at those words, "Ha! Perhaps so, but, you will be gone from here and your precious Vitali!"

Longinus ran up holding his spear and saw Khalid bleeding with the dagger in his heart. He ran to his side, knelt down and cradled his head with his arm and gently lifted it up toward him.

"Khalid! Khalid!"

With his last dying breath, Khalid muttered to Longinus, "Take care of Vitali … she's…." Khalid's eyes rolled back in his head.

Longinus stood up and readied his spear at the Sorcerer. In anger he thrust it at the Sorcerer's face. The Sorcerer covered his face with his cloak and vanished.

Longinus ran back to Khalid and held him tight; he roared a cry so loud it echoed throughout the canyon. Vitali came leaping and nudged Khalid with his nose, he belted out an ear piercing howl of mourning for her master. Justus ran up.

"Father, what happened?"

"The Sorcerer killed him!"

Priscilla came running toward them with Mary by her side. As they got closer, Priscilla saw that Khalid was dead. She stopped and turned Mary around shielding her eyes.

"This is not good for you to see."

Arêtes II ran up. He shook his head sadly at Khalid's dead body and Longinus holding him tight. He hurried over to Priscilla and Mary and led them away.

Priscilla looked back at Longinus and Khalid. Tears streamed down her cheeks and she wept bitterly.

THE REVELATION

The passing of Khalid was a cruel reminder to Priscilla and Longinus that the fight is not against flesh and blood but against principalities and powers of darkness. Longinus had remembered the words of Mary that evil could not be killed with a sword. He fully came to understand exactly what she meant and what she was saying. Prayer and calling on the Lord to intercede was truly the greatest weapon against all manner of evil.

On this day the people had gathered to bury Khalid. It was a sad time but the people supported one another and found comfort in knowing he was with the Lord in paradise. A hand carved rose colored stone marker was placed over his grave with the inscription, "Khalid, A Mighty Servant of The Lord."

Longinus and Priscilla had stayed behind until all the people had left. When the last one was gone, they said their last goodbyes to Khalid and left the burial site. On their walk they remained quiet.

After walking a long way, Longinus opened up and talked of things that lay heavy on his heart.

"Priscilla, it is your lineage he seeks. And all who believe. The Sorcerer is a Satan."

She answered, "No matter what he does, he cannot take one soul out from the hand of the Lord,"

"It is not the soul I fear, it is the flesh. I cannot bear to lose any of you. Not now. Not ever."

"My dear Longinus, you have always known that in the flesh we all must die. By one means or another. Time will pass and one day so shall we."

"You speak such sad words, they are hard to hear."

"I do not say these words to make you sad. I say them so you will understand that you cannot stop what God has ordained to be. You can only accept it."

"I try."

"I know you do."

Priscilla smiled softly and they continued to walk. She spoke freely, "Longinus, you have given me great joy and the marvelous gift of our children. The blessings in watching them grow in the flesh are so many. But this is a small thing. The greatest joy that fills my heart is watching them grow in spirit and in love."

Longinus stopped and pulled Priscilla toward him. He looked longingly into her face. In the hot sun he saw the slightly aged lines at the outer corner of her eyes. He gently touched them with his forefinger. He pulled her closer to him and wrapped his muscular arms around her. He held her tightly next to his chest and bent his head down until his face lay on top of her head. He kissed it and rested his head softly on hers.

He groaned softly, "I can never let you go."

Later that night...

Priscilla and Longinus had gone to bed. Priscilla was fast asleep and Longinus was staring up at the ceiling. Unable to fall asleep he sat up and looked over at his spear by the bedside. He quietly got out of bed and picked up his spear and quietly walked out to the table. He lit a small candle and laid the spear on the table.

He paced for a moment then sat down and stared at the spear. He mumbled to himself under his breath, "How long? What is my purpose?"

He rubbed his forehead and sighed. "Even without the spear I did not age."

He placed his elbows on the table and put his big hand on the side of his head propping it up, then the other hand on the other side and stared at the spear. He started to nod off when suddenly the head of the spear began to glow. Its shining mesmerized him as it radiated brighter and brighter.

He fell into a trancelike state and saw a vision.

In the vision he saw Mary Magdalene coming forward in an open field wearing a beautiful white gown. Her body was glowing with a bright angelic aura. Her arms were out as though she were waiting to embrace someone.

Priscilla appeared and ran toward Mary, they embraced and both ascended upward into the heavens.

Longinus ran to the place where they once stood. He gazed into the heavens where they had ascended then fell to his knees and mourned heavily.

A bellowing voice called out to him telling him to be strong and do not mourn, nor long, but to look at the task set before him.

The spear stopped glowing and Longinus snapped out of the trance.

He jumped out of his chair, frightened and slowly backed away from the spear. Feeling like a trapped animal under attack, his first instinct was to run for he knew he could not fight the destiny of the spear. He leaped to the door and out of the house.

Longinus ran through the winding paths of Petra and up through the treacherous crevices in the highest parts of the carved mountains. He ran and climbed until he reached the highest point and stood silhouetted against the night's moonlit sky.

He reached up to the heavens with his arms outstretched and his fists clenched tight and shouted from the bottom of his lungs, "NOOOOOOO!"

A bellowing voice called out to him, "Longinus, you wrestle not with flesh and blood but with fallen angels and demons of darkness."

"Why me? Why am I to do this?"

The bellowing voice responded, deeper and louder, "You and all in the flesh wrestle against the same evils of darkness."

"How does flesh fight this evil?" he pleaded.

The bellowing voice answered, "Call on my name."

Longinus struggled with his self-will and stubbornly ran from the top of the mountain and into the wilderness. He ran and ran until he dropped from exhaustion. He lay in the dirt panting and gasping for breath.

Out of nowhere, he felt a hand touch his back. An electrifying shiver went down his spine and instantly he was renewed.

Longinus lifted his head and saw the toes of a man protruding outward from a sandal. As he started to get up his eyes were drawn to the entire foot. There was a nail scared hole on the top of the man's foot. He looked up and saw the Nazarene named Jesus.

Jesus spoke to Longinus face to face, "I will not give you more to carry than what you can bear."

Longinus reached out and touched Jesus to see if he was real or imagined. He was real.

Jesus spoke again, "Go and do what you must do. Call on my name and I will come and help you."

Longinus fell prostrate to his knees and bowed his head. "I beg of you, forgive me!"

Jesus reached down and took his hand and lifted him up. "Longinus, when you call my name you will have the army of heaven to help you. Call my name."

Longinus looked at Jesus as he faded away in mid-air. He looked around and touched himself to see if he was awake or asleep. He was awake and returned to his house.

When he entered the house the spear was still on the table. He picked it up and carried it to the room where Priscilla was sleeping and laid it on the floor next to the side of the bed. He crawled in and placed his arm around Priscilla and closed his eyes and fell asleep.

THE AWAKENING

The next morning Longinus awakened, still half asleep in a twilight state, and felt around the bed for Priscilla. He couldn't feel her. As he became more alert he remembered being in the wilderness. Was it a dream or real? Still a bit foggy he recalled meeting Jesus and started to remember everything vividly. Now awake and realizing Priscilla wasn't there, he jumped up and frantically ran out of the room to search for her. He found her in the main room preparing food and let out a gasping sigh of relief.

Priscilla looked at him and asked, "What is wrong?"

Longinus hesitated, not sure how much to tell her and still a little unsure if it was all real or imagined. He was a bit afraid that he might be going a bit mad due to all the things that have happened to him. He reasoned that if he told her what happened last night and she didn't believe him then it would mean it didn't happen and he imagined it. Or something far worse, he might be losing his sound mind.

"Priscilla, last night I had a vision from the spear. I was afraid and ran away in the night. Jesus came to me and told me to call on his name and he will help me with what I must do."

"What is it that you must do?"

Longinus thought and had no answer. He believed he was now going crazy in the head.

"I am not sure. I only know it is to fulfill my destiny. And I do not know if I have gone mad, or if this thing did happen?"

Priscilla answered, "If Jesus had not come to you, then you would not have said it. I believe it is true."

Relieved at hearing Priscilla believed it to have really happened he told her more. "Jesus told me that when I call his name I will have the army of heaven to help me."

Priscilla's heart was filled with joy and her spirit inside was lifted. "Oh Longinus, his blood and his name have conquered death and torn down the gates of hades. In his name you will succeed!"

"Mary has always told me this. It has taken me until now to see it. I have been chosen to protect the lineage of David foremost. First with Mary… now through you and our children."

"Longinus, you were chosen to protect the lineage of David, this I do believe with all my heart. It is your destiny."

"Oh Priscilla, I have been fulfilling my destiny all along and could not see it."

Priscilla smiled at Longinus as her heart leaped with joy in knowing he now understood what he must do and could finally see his past, his present, and his future purpose.

She pulled the hot bread from the fire and happily said, "Come let us pray, giving thanks for all things and eat. The bread is ready."

THE MAGI

Longinus knew in his heart that it was time to learn how to prepare for a battle against a force that can't be seen nor could be fought in the flesh with a sword. There was only one person he knew of that might know of such things. That was Arêtes II.

Longinus went to Arêtes' house and was told he was in the garden in the back. He made his way to the garden and was astounded by its' fragrant aroma and stunning array of the most unusual exotic florals and herbs. An unusual site in the rose colored city of stone. A steady flow of water trickled down through a narrow crevice between two adjoining rose colored cliffs that touched at the top of the mountains rock. The water glistened in the sun.

Arêtes II smiled at Longinus as if he had been waiting for him to arrive. He motioned for Longinus to come and sit on a stone carved seat. Longinus went over and sat down. Arêtes sat across from him, between them was a stone carved stand with a bowl of fresh figs and pomegranates beautifully arranged on top.

Arêtes smiled and asked, "What is it you seek from me?"

Longinus got right to the point as he most always does. "I know my destiny is to protect the lineage of David. But, I do not know what to do next."

Arêtes, answered, "You must be patient. When the next thing to do arises, you will know. Destiny cannot be forced or hurried."

A servant brought them both an urn of juice and poured each a cup. They held up their cups toward one another and drank.

Longinus continued, "I saw the Sorcerer terrified. It was the blood on the spear that he ran from. I have never understood how to wield the spear's power until now."

Arêtes leaned forward with a very stern face, "A Sorcerers power is a lessor power that stems from demons of darkness. To man, it is a frightening. To God, it is useless. Know this."

Longinus huffed boldly, "If I knew where the Sorcerer stayed, I would go and face him."

"Arêtes eyed Longinus as though he were sizing him up. He paused a moment, then as though he had determined Longinus met his approval he shared a valuable source with him.

"There is a Magi that could help you with this. A Sorcerer is a difficult thing to fight. But, he can be fought."

"Can he be killed?" asked Longinus.

Arêtes answered very carefully and with caution, "The demonic realm cannot be killed. But, a powerful host can be."

"How is this done?" asked Longinus, now very interested and leaning in close to hear every word from Arêtes II.

"That depends on how long he has lived and the number of legions he has acquired…and their powers."

Arêtes reached over and took a fig. He held it loosely as he spoke, "The Magi knows how to determine these things."

Arêtes took a bite of the fig.

Longinus eagerly asked, "How do I find this Magi?"

"I have one that can take you to him," answered Arêtes, if you are certain this is what you must do. Are you certain?"

"I am certain," Answered Longinus firmly.

"Prepare for the journey. You shall leave this day," Arêtes put the rest of the fig in his mouth, chewing it he smiled at Longinus. Longinus took a fig and got up, he nodded and popped the fig in his mouth and went to prepare for the journey.

Later at Longinus's house…

Longinus had gathered all of the things for his journey and just finished securing them on the back of his horse. He walked over to Priscilla and gave her a strong hug, then over to Justus and Mary and did the same.

Arêtes II was standing a short distance off holding the reins to a camel that had been loaded with provisions for the journey. A Bedouin man that was to guide Longinus was seated on his camel waiting.

Longinus mounted his horse and trotted over to Arêtes II.

Arêtes II spoke, "Your horse will not due for this trip. I have a camel prepared for you."

THE SPEAR OF DESTINY II

Longinus looked over at the camel. Arêtes nodded. Longinus reluctantly dismounted and pulled his haversack from his horse. He got up on the camel.

Arêtes II smiled. "Avraham will show you the way. It is not far, but the land is a dry wilderness."

"Thank you Arêtes. You have helped me greatly."

Longinus and Avraham headed out and the others all watched them leave until they were out of sight.

Some time later, in the wilderness at night...

Avraham and Longinus had made a fair distance after riding way into the night. They stopped to make camp. As they prepare the camp, Avraham started to share some interesting facts about the Magi they sought.

"The Magi has a lot of powers like a Sorcerer," said Avraham in a mystic tone, "He can stir up many wonders. He can appear and disappear."

Longinus asked, "What does a Magi take for his fee? Arêtes II told me when I find him, we will work that out. I'm curious."

Avraham laughed.

"He said that did he? The Magi needs nothing. It is your mission that will either entice him to help or have him send you on your way."

"My mission is to rid us of the evil Sorcerer that I have been told is also called the Old Man."

"You can only wait and see," said Avraham as he laid out his bed roll for the night.

Longinus looked a bit confused. Thinking always made him exhausted. He busied himself with bedding down the camel. When he was finished, he grabbed his bedroll and had a few more questions.

He spoke out to Avraham, "If the Magi..." he looked and Avraham was fast asleep.

Longinus was disappointed, but knew he better not wake him. He rolled out his bedding and lay down for the night, and closed his eyes to fall asleep.

THE SORCERER'S DESIRE

The Sorcerer was in his lair looking through scrolls of spells. "Now where is the spell to acquire the possession of a fallen angel? I need more power."

The old man tossed several books aside and kept searching through others. He mumbled to himself, "I gained a lot of demonic legions when I possessed Nero. I wonder, is that enough?"

He pulled another book out and searched through it. "Aha!" he exclaimed, "Here it is!" He read closely.

"Curses! I need more legions of demons to gain access past Beelzebub for this!" The Sorcerer pondered what to do.

"I hate dealing with the heads of legions," he grumbled, "It is so much easier to be in the flesh of one in power and have the Prince send them to me. There is no time to be trapped in a body now....unless?"

The Sorcerer picked up another book and read closely.

"That is it! I can possess a body of flesh and exit its' confines by causing the host to commit suicide. That should be no problem," He cackled as he clapped his hands with sinister glee.

The old man put his finger to his chin and tapped it as he pondered.

"Now who shall I possess? I need someone that has many legions of demons. But legions don't give up their host easily...what can be done here? Let me think on this."

The Sorcerer decided to summon some assistance. "Oh demons of Diana come to me now."

Instantly his demons of Diana appeared.

"Yes, Master. Why do you summon us?"

"I am in need of a body that is filled with legions of demons, but, it must be one I can control in the flesh, even to death by the hosts own hands. Where can I find such a host?"

The head demon of Diana laughed, "What you seek is a war with the under- world. No legions of demons so great would ever give up their host by its' own hand. For it would also be suicide for them, sending them back to wander aimlessly within the confines of hades."

The Old Man is not pleased with what he has heard. "Find me an answer. Or I will cast you out and replace you with others!"

The head demon shook a bit, "You have found your own answer, Master. If you are more powerful than what is inside the host when you enter it, you can control who stays and who goes,"

"Aha! Indeed. I can eliminate any opposing legions within the host by commanding the powerful force of my own personal loyal demons, such as yourselves, to cast them out for me!"

The head demon added, "Actually, that will only be so "if" your demons are more powerful."

The Sorcerer glared at the head Demon of Diana, "Then make that become so!"

"Yes, Master."

THE ENCOUNTER

The next day, Longinus and Avraham are deep in the Wilderness of Zin. They have come to a place in the middle of a deep cavern surrounded by protruding clefts jetting out from the jagged walls of mountain. The heat radiated from the hot sands creating a mirage of water ahead, teasing them as their mouths parched for thirst.

Avraham looked over and pointed, "There…in the rock. The Magi has a place."

They proceed to the place where Avraham believed the Magi was. They come close to a place in the rock and a peel of thunder boomed, echoing off the canyon walls, resounding as though it was coming from all sides at once.

A powerful voice called out, "Come no further, state your purpose."

Longinus shouted back, "Show yourself!"

A lightning bolt struck the ground directly in front of them. The camels waver and jolt. Longinus and Avraham steady them.

Longinus called out, "I seek a powerful Magi."

The powerful voice bellowed out, "All Magi are powerful."

"I seek you, the good Magi."

The voice answered, "Good Magi? Bad Magi? How do you know what one I am?"

Longinus proclaimed, "Arêtes II said you could help. If you were bad, he would not have sent me."

The Magi slowly came forth from a place in the rock. His appearance was that of an average sized man. A black scarf was wrapped around his head, covering his entire face leaving only his eyes peering out through a narrow slit, with a black turban on his head. He wore a black silky shirt and harem pants, with a black robe trimmed in silver thread that flowed to the ground and horn toed boots.

He smiled, "I believe you know I hold a power," He eyed Longinus's spear. "I see you hold a greater power," The Magi pulled down the black cloth, to reveal his face and bowed.

"At your service Longinus."

Longinus looked at Avraham. Avraham shrugged his shoulders and shook his head gesturing he did not have any answer for this. Longinus looked back over to the Magi.

"How do you know my name? And how do you know I hold a great power?"

"I have heard the legend of the one named Longinus who holds the spear that has the blood of the great Master upon it. It is a blood I must obey."

"Can you help me find the Sorcerer, the one they call the Old Man?"

"Aaah, an easy one to find. I well know of him," answered the Magi, "Come."

The Magi motioned for them to follow him. They dismounted their camels and followed the Magi through the entrance in the rock.

The Magi asked, "So, you have come far? Or not?"

Longinus answered, "The destiny has been long; our journey to find you here has not."

The Magi grinned. "I see you are versed in how to get the attention of a Magi."

Feeling he has found favor, Longinus cuts right to the point, "Can you tell me the Sorcerers life span? His number of demons and their powers?"

"You boldly ask a lot. Finding him is one thing," answered the Magi, "Assessing his power is another."

Longinus turned to leave and started walking.

The Magi looked puzzled at Longinus's abruptness. How strange, he thought, and then he shouted at him, "I did not tell you I could not answer. Why are you in such a hurry?"

Longinus stopped and turned around. He answered as he walked back to the Magi, "I have no time to waste. Not yours, nor mine. Will you help me destroy this Sorcerer?"

The Magi responded, "You are aware...this task you believe is so easily taken on ... will bring you directly into the gates of hades, are you not?"

"I am aware."

The Magi smiled then became very serious.

"Your battle is not with flesh and blood but with the powers within the gates of Hades that oppose all good."

Longinus raised his spear. "The power upon this spear broke down those gates."

The Magi thought and paced. He looked at Longinus and thought about his arrogance and impatience as though he were speaking to someone telepathically.

"Will he be able to listen in order to learn? He has already acted foolishly impulsive. Will I be wasting my time with this one? But he does need directing or he'll create a big disturbance in the underworld. Indeed, and this world as well. I guess we must."

The Magi came to his decision.

"I will only help you because I must. The blood on your spear speaks to me. I obey it, not you. Understood?"

Longinus nodded.

BEELZEBUB'S WARNING

Meanwhile back at the Sorcerers Lair...

The Sorcerer is in deep meditation. He is now seeking to find a man in the flesh that possesses as great a power as he has. His desire is focused on how to possess that body and wield a double power so he can acquire the possession of a fallen angel.

Inside the images within his mind's eye he saw a powerful Magi in the wilderness of Zin. This one possessed the power he was seeking. But, how was he going to achieve this task?

As he anxiously thought of how to approach this act, he thought of none other than the Prince of all Demons, the great and ominous Lord of the Flies – Beelzebub.

He eagerly summoned him and anticipated his arrival with bubbling zeal.

Beelzebub was the overlord of spreading belief in false gods, starting wars, fanning the flames of lust, and most of all, he was the master of possessing human bodies to carry out horrific acts.

Beelzebub was exactly the one he needed to consult to get his fallen angel. He did not hold a lot of confidence in what his Demons of Diana had to say.

After a short while, Beelzebub appeared like a fat, greenish ghoul with long ram horns that protruded out from his forehead, he was as tall as the room and kept getting bigger and bigger until he enveloped within it. Then POOF, he diminished to the size of a man and shapeshifted into a muscular hulk, thick boned with large hands and oversized feet, with a strong jaw and handsomely chiseled features. He was bare foot and bare chested wearing black haram pants, with a silver sash around his waist. He looked at the Sorcerer.

"What do ya want?"

The Sorcerer presented his proposal, "Beelzebub, I have found a Magi in the Wilderness of Zin that holds a great power equal to my own. How can I possess his flesh and gain his power?"

"That's the Magi with the power of a fallen one."

The Sorcerer jumped with glee. "Yes, yes! How do I possess his flesh?"

Beelzebub laughed, "I'd like to see ya do that. Fun battle to watch. Let me know when you go for it."

The Sorcerer angered for being mocked defended his stance, "This Magi is no greater than I. He is no match for my legions."

Beelzebub gave the Sorcerer a dirty stare.

"Go on do it. Enjoy the chaos. That fallen one the Magi has seeks to redeem himself by doing heavens bidding."

The Sorcerer thought for a moment. "I see. It is none the less a fallen one, is it not?"

"Sure. But he's not one to mess with. He's serious about his stupid desire to change his eternity."

"I see," Said the Sorcerer.

"There's noth'in I hate more than a fallen that jumps ship 'cause he thinks we're gonna lose," complained Beelzebub.

"That is disgusting. Tell me, how hard would it be to get a fallen that desires not to be redeemed?"

Beelzebub burst out laughing, "Man you're full of it today ain't ya."

"Actually, I'm quite serious."

"Ain't no way in Hades any fallen's gonna wanna get inside a sorcerer. It's the other way around fella"

The Sorcerer heard enough of Beelzebub's negative outlook, "Very well. You have been most helpful."

Beelzebub snickered then disappeared.

The Sorcerer was so obsessed with his desire to possess a fallen angel he ignored Beelzebub's warnings.

"Beelzebub can't possibly believe a fallen angel would be interested in redemption. Especially if all he does is sickening good deeds through a Magi in the wilderness. I'm sure he has tired of all that by now."

The Sorcerer pulled an ancient scroll from the top of the table. "I will see what can be done. Everyone has a price."

He rolled it out and placed it in front of him and began to search through it line by line with his pointy finger dragging across each word.

"Now… how can I entice him?"

OF DEMONS AND FLESH

The Magi had agreed to help Longinus with his task of finding the Sorcerer but he knew there was much to teach him before he could successfully enter into a battle against one with such command over evil principalities and powers. He also knew that Longinus was a stubborn, impulsive soul who needed a subtle way of instructing. He had decided to return with them using the journey as a means to get through to Longinus and show him what he must learn; for there was much he did not know and he was ill prepared to battle the Sorcerer.

Longinus, Avraham, and the Magi are now on their camels returning to Petra and have reached the outskirts.

The Magi looked ahead sizing up how much further before they reached their destination. "I could have just willed us to Petra and saved us much time and toil."

Longinus was not amused by the Magi's comment.

"Save your magic for finding the Sorcerer."

The Magi answered, "The Sorcerer is in his lair. He will be summoning me shortly."

Longinus curiously eyed the Magi then asked, "How do you know this?"

"Beelzebub whispered for me to beware for the Sorcerer, known as 'The Old Man' wishes to possess me for my power."

Longinus looked at the Magi as though he were making that all up. He sneered arrogantly, "Just why would Beelzebub do that?"

The Magi sensed Longinus was in nonbelief of his words and wondered if he should even answer him. He refrained from his own pettiness and answered, "Because Beelzebub answers to the fallen angels. Even the one that resides in me."

Longinus gave the Magi a curious look. "Oh."

They rode along, then Longinus had another question, "Has Beelzebub whispered how old, strong, or powerful the Sorcerer is?"

The Magi laughed out loud at Longinus's persistent need to know that answer.

Longinus insisted, "Well, has he?"

The Magi decided to answer him hoping it would put an end to his asking, and hoping even more it would not lead to a mountain of more questions.

"The Sorcerer has been around since the time of Jannes and Jambres. His powers are satanic and come from centuries of possessing bodies. He is indeed very powerful."

Longinus was surprised to finally get an answer and was eager to know more.

He asked, "How is this so?"

The Magi answered, "When the host body dies in the flesh, he is free to leave it and all the demons stay with him. He has become a great and powerful host for evil."

Longinus boasted, "He is terrified by the blood on my spear,"

The Magi sensed that Longinus was thinking the spear was all he needed and nothing more. He was concerned with this over confident sense of himself.

"That is the only thing demons fear. The blood is from a principality and power greater than theirs. They don't want to battle that. They grow in strength by feeding off the flesh."

Longinus looked puzzled, "I don't understand?"

The Magi explained, "The flesh is very weak. Demons play with man's mortal nature through manipulating their thoughts, emotions and fears to do their bidding," He paused a moment then continued, "You see, they can do nothing unless they possess a host to do their bidding for them. Once inside they take over eating and chewing away at every thread of a mortal's sense of worth, convincing them that they are to evil to ever be redeemed.

"Demons seek to destroy the natural will to do what is right. Instead, they take control and magnify every carnal desire, pushing temptations at them from all directions.

"Once they take possession of a mortal's self- will it is almost impossible in the flesh to take it back. It takes the power of the blood on your spear. That is the only thing that can end their stay inside the flesh once they have taken it over."

Longinus was angered at hearing how the demons work inside the flesh. How a thing that could not be seen could destroy so much.

"They are like an angry wind that cannot be seen but can blow a house apart," Stated Longinus.

"That is one way to see it. Yes," Said the Magi.

"How can I destroy these demons?"

The Magi answered, "Can you destroy the wind?"

A frustrated and impatient Longinus retorted, "We're not talking about the wind, we speak of demons!"

The Magi answered, "Is there any difference?"

Suddenly, Longinus's eyes widened. The Magi's riddle was starting to make sense; he remembered Mary Magdalene's words and said, "I was told that evil spirits were cursed to roam the earth like the wind, seeking to possess empty vessels. At the time I did not understand this thing."

"How do you understand it now?" asked the Magi.

"I see the empty vessels are bodies that allow demons in to stay and do great harm and," he paused for a moment in his thoughts, "sometimes they enter to harm the innocent, as in sickness."

"So what can be done to fight a demon?" asked the Magi.

A bit dumbfounded, Longinus reasoned, "I saw Mary Magdalene tell them to go out from the sick people and they were made well. So, it seems you just tell them to go."

The Magi took a breath and closed his eyes, "Well, that is one way to look at it. But there is more to this than your eyes understood."

"I know what my eyes saw!" Longinus quipped like an impatient child.

The Magi gave him a stern look and remained silent until Longinus became uncomfortable.

"In all my days I have never found one as foolish and stubborn as this one! I will help him no longer," He spoke as though he were addressing someone other than Longinus.

Longinus felt his heart drop like an anchor. He did not know what to say.

A voice was heard coming from the Magi, but the Magi's lips never moved, "His foolish, stubbornness is not why he was chosen. You must teach him how to cast evil spirits from the flesh."

"If I must," Answered the Magi reluctantly to what appeared to be himself.

"To just cast them from the flesh," said the Magi as he shook his head, "They just roam the earth and find another body to possess."

"Can they ever be bound so they do not wander?" asked Longinus.

The Magi answered, "The name of the one whose blood is on the spear, is the only name that can bind them. It has the power to send them all back to hades."

In hearing that, Longinus remembered more vividly what Mary did, she bound them and cast them back to Hades in the Masters name, he then recalled Jesus telling him to call on his name and he will send the armies of heaven to fight for him, stressing that he must call on his name first.

Longinus raised his spear high in the air, "I have both the power of the name and the power of the blood."

The Magi, unaware of Longinus's encounter with Jesus, shook his head.

"All who believe have that same power. That is not enough."

Longinus was no longer sure if he could trust the Magi. He thought he was speaking like a demon now.

"You no longer speak like a follower. You sound like a Sorcerer playing with my mind."

The Magi defended his words fast, "I say these things because believing is one thing, laying down your life is another. Standing firm and fighting back with the power of the blood strong enough to cast these out and bind them takes preparation."

"I was told by Jesus, himself, to call his name and he would send me his army of angels to fight with me. He did not say I had to make it all so hard. He said just call on my name."

The Magi has tired of trying to explain and frustrated that Longinus did not understand the depth of what he was teaching. He spoke one last time, "You must surrender all of your will to him and let him direct you. Preparation for a task like this takes much fasting and prayer. If you have not done this, you are not ready to fight the underworld."

Longinus was silent. They continued along on their camels.

A MIGHTY DJINN

The Sorcerer had kept himself busy aggressively researching spells and incantations. He now believed he had found a fool proof way of going around the problem of capturing the fallen angel within the Magi.

He was in his lair, busily placing stones in a circle and preparing to conjure up a Djinn; an all-powerful one to do his bidding. He stepped inside the circle and held out his arms. He strategically turned around slowly two times, then turned back the other way 'one and a half times' slowly. Then, he turned the other way one time slowly and stopped. He closed his eyes and began to chant.

"Powers of darkness, masters of sin, bring unto me the most powerful Djinn!"

At once, the room began to vibrate in the most volatile manner. The entire lair shook and the rows of potions, rattled violently, clanging together, sending many of them crashing to the floor. A black cloud filled the room until it became totally darkened, followed by a terrible high pitched screeching; then another and another layering into a shrill cacophony of unbearable sound.

When the rumbling ceased and the black cloud lifted, the room became silent and a DJINN appeared, standing with his arms folded. He was huge. The left side of his body was flesh color and the right side was bright blue. He wore jewels around his neck, and huge rings on each of his six fingers layered to his knuckles. There was a thick, shiny brass ring in his nose and layers of chains crisscrossing around his torso of various sizes.

The Djinn spoke in a deep thundering tone, "Speak your purpose."

The Sorcerer commanded with a sinister tone, "I desire you to go with me to possess the flesh of a Magi."

The Djinn answered angrily, "You summoned me for that? I waste not my time to do what you can do on your own." The

Djinn looked as though he was preparing to leave and the Sorcerer shouted, "Wait!" The Djinn stopped.

The Sorcerer explained, "This is the Magi that hosts a fallen angel."

The Djinn looked at the Old Man and contemplated for a moment as he rubbed his chin with his hand.

"I know this one. It is not wise to do this deed."

The Sorcerer snapped back at the Djinn, "I did not summon you to tell me what is or is not wise. You will go with me."

The Djinn nodded, "So be it. Summon me when you go."

The Djinn whirled around and disappeared. The Sorcerer was delighted as he picked up his sphere and peered into it. An image of the Magi appeared on a camel in the outskirts of Petra with Longinus traveling next to him. The Sorcerer cackled out a long, deep, devious laugh. He continued to gaze into the sphere for a long while, and then put it down.

"I will have the Djinn take care of the Magi. Now let me think. What will weaken the Enigma? Oh yes, his precious Priscilla."

The Sorcerer quickly conjured up six demons of plague. They responded, "Master, what is your wish?"

"There is a woman in Petra named Priscilla. Go to her now and cause a great illness to befall her."

"Yes Master."

The demons vanish and the Sorcerer burst into an explosive high pitched cackle so loud and devilish it cracked the cavernous wall of his lair, shifting its foundation causing the red haze from the five dark tunnel openings to no longer align, scrambling the shape of the pentagram into a haphazard mist. He curiously looked at it.

"My, my... that has never happened." He thought a moment curiously, "Is that a good omen or a bad?" He started to open his Codex to check, then hesitated, "There's no time for this now."

He turned and disappeared.

THE FINAL SHOWDOWN

The Sorcerer suddenly appeared in the outskirts of Petra. He looked all about at his surroundings with a sinister smirk on his face as he anticipated the evil act that he was about to execute.

He stood still and slowly shape shifted into the body of a young woman. He felt his arms and smiled.

Next he conjured up a donkey loaded up with heavy bundles on his back. He cackled softly and picked up a heavy stone. He swung it back hard and thrust it forward breaking the donkey's leg. The donkey hawed out painfully.

The Sorcerer, now appearing as a young woman stood there by the suffering animal and waited.

"They will be along any minute now," She said.

A little while later…

In the distance Longinus and the Magi spy a young woman crying by her donkey that is braying out in terrible pain. They quickly approach her.

The young woman crying pitifully lifted up her face to Longinus and pleaded, "Sir, my donkey has hurt his leg and I don't know what to do."

Longinus asked, "Woman, how far do you have to go?"

She answered, "I go to Petra. But, look and see … my donkey has broken its' leg. My things are too heavy and too many for me to carry on foot."

Longinus started to get down from his camel and the Magi motioned for him to halt.

The Magi warned, "This is a Sorcerer's trick."

Longinus was bewildered at hearing that. He looked at the crying young woman which was one of his biggest weaknesses. He was just wired to always help a damsel in distress and this young woman was in distress, or so it appeared. He was torn in what to do. He glanced at the Magi, then at the young woman.

The woman pleaded, "This is no trick. Help me. I beg you."

Longinus looked again at the Magi, then at the young woman. He reasoned a moment then got down from his camel. He walked toward the woman without his spear.

The Magi sighed and rolled his eyes.

Longinus no sooner bent over to check the donkey's leg and the woman cackled in the evil voice of the Sorcerer. Startled, Longinus looked up at her while with the voice of the Sorcerer, she summoned the Djinn.

"Powers of darkness, masters of sin, bring unto me the most powerful Djinn!"

Instantly the Djinn appeared towering above the canyon walls.

The Sorcerer in the body of the young woman commanded the Djinn with a sinister shout, "Get his spear now!"

The Djinn reached over and picked up the spear from the weapon holder on the side of Longinus's camel. In his massive hand it looked like a small splinter.

Longinus stood at the ready with his sword prepared to fight the Djinn.

The woman spun around and shape shifted into the Sorcerer. Believing he was now invincible and his evil plan was about to be completed, he jumped up and down with glee laughing his evil laugh.

"Now, where was I? Oh yes. The Djinn," He looked over calmly then yelled, "Now kill the Magi with the spear!"

The Djinn, towering over the Canyon, reduced his size to around 15 foot tall. The spear now fit in his hand, but the size of the Djinn made it look more like he was wielding an arrow more than a spear.

The Djinn leaned over and picked up the Magi from his camel and placed him up on his shoulder.

Longinus shook his head fiercely and tried to refocus his eyes. He could not make sense of what he was seeing. The Djinn with the Magi on his shoulder, the woman now the Sorcerer. His own folly of not listening to the Magi and not calling on the name of the Lord, all these things and more flashed through his mind in a flash.

Meanwhile, the Sorcerer grew furious. "What are you doing!!?" He yelled angrily at his Djinn.

The Djinn answered, "I told you it would not be wise to pursue this Magi. You told me you did not summon me to know what was wise or not wise."

The Sorcerer shouted, "Speak clearly. What do you mean?"

The Djinn answered, "You summoned me, the most powerful Djinn, whose master is this most powerful Magi."

The Sorcerer screamed, "AARRG!" He desperately tried to change the sour direction this attack was going. He at least wanted to secure a peaceful retreat for himself. So he sought to reason with the Djinn, "But you said you would go with me!"

The Djinn answered, "And so...I am here. I did not tell you what I would do. You failed to ask that question."

The Djinn handed the spear to the Magi and the Magi tossed it to Longinus. Longinus caught the spear and lunged it at the Sorcerer. The Sorcerer turned to spin and disappear but the Magi held out his hand and froze the Sorcerer between time and space.

The Sorcerers demons screeched out pleading for the Magi's Fallen Angel to have mercy on them.

Longinus stood in the face of the Sorcerer and readied his spear. Simultaneously the Magi released his spell, unfreezing the Sorcerer.

Longinus thundered out from the bottom of his lungs, " Jesus in your name like you promised, send me the army of Heaven to fight this wicked one!"

He thrust his spear, piercing it deep into the Sorcerer's heart.

The Sorcerer let out a chilling wale and cursed Longinus with all sorts of vile utterances as he writhed in pain.

Longinus thrust in his sword deeper and twisted it, pushing and twisting until it went clear through.

The Sorcerer bent his head forward and uttered the most horrifying words Longinus could ever bear to hear, "Your precious Priscilla is dying from my demons of plague. Your life without her will be an unbearable hell."

Longinus pulled his spear from the Sorcerers heart. Instantly the Sorcerer aged rapidly. He turned wrinkled, leathery, and hideous to look at. His body cracked and fell apart as he crumbled into dust and blended into the sands.

The demons screeched and pleaded.

"Spare us! Let us to go into another. Please spare us. Do not send us bound to Hades."

Longinus felt no pity for them.

He shouted in a deep, authoritative voice, "In the name of the Lord Jesus and his blood on the spear, I cast you back, bound to the chains of Hades!"

The demons let out howling screeches. The ground quaked and opened a deep fissure; they screamed and hissed as they were sucked into the gaping hole, cast back into the deep recesses of Hades.

The Magi shouted to Longinus, "Go to Priscilla! She calls for you."

The Magi waved his hand and instantly Longinus vanished.

HADES' LOVELESS ARMS

Beelzebub was standing in front of a massive whirling portal waiting as though he were expecting something to come out from it. He had just watched the entire showdown through the means of remote viewing in his mind's eye.

He counted, "3...2...1."

Suddenly, a hoard of howling, screeching evil spirits came rumbling out from the portal into Hades chambers bound in glowing translucent chains that secured their entire bodies, starting at their feet wrapping upward in a spiral to their necks.

Beelzebub hollered to a legion of about a hundred ghoulish demons with black leathery, wrinkled skin swarming on top of each other chattering their teeth unceasingly.

"Put'em in there," He pointed to a fiery pit full of screaming evil spirits."

The ghoulish demons grabbed hold of the bound spirits and began the task of casting them into the fiery pit.

"Now, let's see, this'll be his first time so he should be coming right about.....," suddenly, the Old Man came hurling through the whirling portal, "...NOW."

The Old Man rolled out from the portal and on to the stone floor naked. He was ugly to look at with shriveled skin, and chunks of flesh missing exposing his bones and jaw teeth.

"Well, ya didn't listen," Beelzebub said very disgusted, "Now I gotta figure out how to replace ya."

"Send me back out," Begged the Sorcerer.

"Ha! You know noth'in of how this works, do ya?"

The old man shivered and covered his private parts with his hands.

"Fools that don't listen stay here. Get used to it."

The old man's eyes widened in horror.

Beelzebub reached down and grabbed the old man up by his neck and pulled him close about one inch away from his face and said in a creepy voice, "What do ya got to say about redemption now?"

The old man choking, made a desperate plea, "I know you have power with Hades over the dead to redeem who you choose for a price."

He threw him back to the ground and sneered, "What's your price?"

The Old Man covered his private parts with his hands and stood up on his feet looking wretched and fearful, but tried his best to appear empirical.

"I have thought long of the wonder how a mortal's greatest weakness is a lie within his soul. For when mortals are deceived by what appears to be true, but is actually a lie, they will fight to the death to uphold such deceit not knowing at all that it is not true."

"Not impressed. That's the whole point here," Scoffed Beelzebub.

"But I can offer Hades millions of souls by performing great deceit against those that follow the one who tore down the gates of these walls."

"I'm listening."

"I can change the words he spoke into enticing charms for itching ears."

"Ya know we're not allowed to touch the words. Bad idea."

"It's not the words that will be touched...it is the interpretation of the words that will place the lie in the soul. Little by little, the truth will be left out and soon, all they follow will be of the interpretation of devils."

Beelzebub was impressed. "Gotta hand it to ya, but Simon beat ya to it."

"True, but, Simon is no longer alive and when he was, he was not effective against the power of the Apostle's influence. Especially Peter, sadly, he overpowered Simon's demons in prayer. That was a sight to see. I was really rooting for him too. He did so well at first. He conjured the demons and made that glorious spectacle in the air ascending to heaven.

"There he was just soaring along, flying higher and higher, when Peter started praying to cast out his demons and BAM! Out

THE SPEAR OF DESTINY II

they went and Simon plummeted like a rock to the ground. What a mess that was."

"Oh yea, that. He went straight to the Lake of Fire, Michael escorted 'em… never came through the portal. Demons are still scared of Peter 'cause of Simon, none dare speak his name."

"That is my point. Followers must never know they have such power over the underworld."

"Crap!" Beelzebub had not considered that. He drifted off in his own thoughts remembering the day the son of God threw open the gates of Hell by his command. He looked at the place where the gates were tore down and recalled that horrible moment.

He thought of how his mere presence made Satan and Hades tremble and they had no power at all against his name nor his word. The captured souls were shouting and praising and they were all freed.

"Paradise", he mumbled, "He took 'em to Paradise."

The sheer idea that the Apostles were showing others the way to overcome death through that blood was terrifying.

Beelzebub looked at the Old Man who had been chattering the entire time.

"…or they will be, they still call him out as we speak. They even scribed his deceit into their Holy Scrolls. I WILL be effective."

The Old Man was clueless that Beelzebub did not have his undivided attention and kept rambling, "I will place the ultimate lie in the soul. One so great men will kill to defend it for all generations."

Beelzebub looked at him in a surly manner, "What tha hell are ya talk'en about? I hate it when useless fools flap their jaws waste'n my time. Just how ya gonna do any different than Simon?"

The Old Man answered, "Simon merely laid the ground work. I will create a great age of shadows that will usher in a new authority. Once all the Jewish Apostles are gone and out of the WAY…," he paused and giggled on his play of words, "I will confound the interpretations through means of translation in the manner of the tower of Babel."

"Old Man ya sound like an idiot."

"Beelzebub, I deplore you, when men are left with no memory of customs, nor meanings of the language, they will be forced to have those I empower tell them what it means. There will be great burnings of their little precious writings of the Way."

Beelzebub snarled, "That'll take too much time. Besides, they've already burned a bunch a stuff."

"Are you willing to risk more of the same use of Holy Power in the likes that was done by Peter? Might I remind you that I possessed Nero at the time and know full well of our limitations."

Beelzebub made a dismissing sound and rolled his eyes.

The Old Man continued.

"Are you aware the followers have gone abroad spreading their ideas...it grows fast. The only way now is to usurp them. I will build on what Simon had called his trinity in the manner of the Queen of Heaven- his new universal glory worship of which he was the god and founder of. And might I add, Rome had very much liked."

Beelzebub had a different opinion and argued, "I say kill'em all! And fast!"

The Old Man, having nothing to lose, stood his ground and got louder, "And so do I, but, are you aware that as we speak Rome has issued a decree to kill all the Jews of the Way and all who spoke against Simon and his Universal worship?"

Beelzebub barked back, "Yea, so what's your point?"

"There is one big flaw to that." The Old man paused as if he had a gem of guarded knowledge he might not tell Beelzebub unless he asked.

"Don't toy with me!" boomed Beelzebub, "What's the flaw?"

"The flaw is that there has been a great conversion in the Isles and in many nations not under Roman dictates. Non Jewish now follow the Way. Since you can't kill everybody, my plan will take care of this pesky matter and..." He paused a moment then added, "We still kill those who get in our WAY. Hee hee."

Beelzebub hedging a bit asked, "Your lie in the soul stuff, how far can ya push it?"

"Oh it's endless. Imagine what can be done when no one believes there is a Hades? No fallen angels? No such thing as demons, no Beelzebub? No nasty lake of fire? Imagine there is no god so what's the point of anything? Live for today for tomorrow you die." The Sorcerer looked inquisitively at Beelzebub, "Are you seeing my point yet?"

Beelzebub's face grimaced, it was obvious he was about to say something he did not want to say.

"Ya got one chance. Only because of all you did with Nero. If ya blow it, you're done, back here worse than ya are now. Got that?"

"Indeed," replied the old man as he took a deep sigh of relief.

"Now about my clothes and flesh…"

I WILL SEE YOU AGAIN

Longinus suddenly appeared in the bedroom of Priscilla. He had not expected to see two women tending to her. One was placing a cold compress on her forehead and the other was adding a powder to the bowl they were dipping it in. Justus and Mary were sitting beside her bed. They were very distraught and their eyes swollen from crying.

Longinus was beside himself at the sight of his children and Priscilla laying almost lifeless in her bed. He ran over to her bedside, not knowing what to do or how to help. His mind was flashing back between the loss of his beloved and the loss of Mary as he put his arms around Priscilla lifting her head up and off the pillow. He embraced her tenderly kissing her cheek. Priscilla smiled but was too weak to embrace him back.

Longinus tried hard not to break down, but he could not hold back the tears swelling up in the corners of his of his eyes. He moaned pitifully. "No! No! This shall not be. In the name of the Lord and by his blood- be well!"

The women backed away and motioned with their hands at Justus and Mary to come and leave the room with them. They got up slowly and quietly followed the women out of the room. At the doorway, Mary longingly looked back. She didn't want to leave, but the woman whispered something in her ear and Mary reluctantly followed her out.

Longinus stared longingly into Priscilla's eyes. He stroked her skin softly.

Priscilla tried to talk, but her mouth was too dry. Longinus eyed a pale of fresh water on the small table. He quickly went and dipped a ladle full and brought it to Priscilla. "Take a sip", he told her. Priscilla took a sip and then another. She motioned to Longinus that it was enough. Longinus drank what was left in the ladle and placed it down on the side of the bed.

In a fragile, weak voice Priscilla spoke, "An angel has come to me and told me to fear not. It is my time."

"No Priscilla, my love. This cannot be." Quipped Longinus.

Priscilla continued, "It is God's will. Please take care of Justus and Mary. The Lord has a great plan for them."

"Priscilla, you will be well. You have to be well." Tears streamed down his sun scorched face. He could no longer contain his sorrow and clung desperately to her like a grieving child.

Priscilla was limp in his arms. Suddenly she smiled and extended out her arm past Longinus as though to touch someone, "Oh mother, you have come. And father. Do you see them Longinus?"

Longinus looked over to where Mary was holding out her arm and hand and saw no one. But, he answered, "Yes, I see them."

Priscilla offered up a faint smile. "You see."

She closed her eyes and Longinus panicked. "Priscilla, Priscilla."

She opened her eyes halfway and spoke ever so faintly and feeble, "I go to be with my Lord. The day will come and I will see you, Justus and Mary again. I promise you."

Priscilla's eyes rolled back in their sockets and she ceased to breathe. Longinus gently closed her lids and held tight to her lifeless body weeping and mourning heavily.

After a long while had passed, Arêtes II entered the room. He stood in the doorway for a moment, then approached Longinus and gently placed his hand on Longinus's shoulder.

"Your children need you. You must go to them."

"Longinus reluctantly got up from Priscilla's bedside, and slowly went into the other room.

Justus and Mary ran to their father and embraced him. They stood holding each other tight, weeping and grieving together.

The next day...

Longinus was still grieving bitterly. He composed himself and entered the common room. His children were at the table in sorrow, still in deep mourning.

Longinus addressed the children, "Come."

Longinus sat down on a flatbed couch. His children walked over to him and sat one on each side. He placed his massive arms around them and drew them close.

He spoke to them in a somber tone, "There are things you must know."

Justus and Mary listened closely.

Longinus began to explain a serious matter that he believed they must now know before another moment went by, for life was fleeting and unpredictable. He was about to tell them a very important thing that they must always remember and pass on to their children.

"You are of the line of King David from the tribe of Benjamin. Your Grandmother was the Great Supreme Female Magdalene of the tribe."

Justus and Mary were very still and listened attentively.

Longinus looked at Justus and said, "Justus, your mother said your lineage is destined to produce great kings."

He then looked at Mary and said, "And great queens."

Longinus pointed to his spear leaned up against the wall across the room.

"We have duty to the one whose blood is on the spear." A tear fell from his eye, "Our lives have changed. But, it is our destiny. We must be strong. Your mother wanted that for us."

Justus lifted his head and spoke like a man, "I will be strong."

Mary understood and shared, "Mother told me of our lineage when she lay sick. She told me we must be careful not to ever tell anyone. Romans seek to kill the entire lineage of David. Is this true papa?"

Longinus sighed deeply and answered, "Yes, this is true."

Justus was surprised to hear that and was concerned.

"Why would Romans want to kill those of David?"

"Justus, I truly do not know," Said Longinus, "But I promise you, I will find out why they do this thing."

A few days later at the burial...

There was a crowd of people gathered to mourn the passing of Priscilla, almost all the people of Petra were there. It was hard for Longinus to say his goodbyes, but he managed to hold his emotions intact for the sake of his children. He had to be strong for them. They needed the comforting now and he made sure he was there for them.

They placed her coffin into a sepulcher and Arêtes II had several men of Petra roll a large stone in front of its opening. Longinus, Justus and Mary watched as it rolled in front hiding the view of the coffin and locked into place. It was a strong sign of the finality of Priscilla's passing.

Longinus remembered the words of the Nazarene on the cross before he gave up his life, and said those same words to his children. He took each by the hand and said, "It is finished." They walked away from the sepulcher together.

Justus asked, "What will we do now father?"

Longinus looked at Justus and Mary. "I have thought and I have prayed on this. We must go on a long journey across the sea, to a place where your grandmother, Mary, spent many years." Longinus started to choke up and took a moment to grip his composure.

He continued, "It is a place where your mother also found great joy. We must find your mother's brother. That is a good place for us to begin to find him."

THE LINEAGE CONTINUES

Three days later, Longinus, Justus, and Mary were packed and ready to leave Petra. Their time in the rose colored city was finished and now Longinus was ready to begin a new journey. A journey with no clear map to guide him, only bits and pieces of Priscilla's past and the stories she had shared. But his quest was clear and burned in his heart. He must find the children's uncle, the brother of Priscilla and protect the lineage of David.

Many people had gathered to see them off, and to make sure they had everything they needed. Longinus was not used to all this type of fuss, or perhaps he never paid attention to it. Priscilla always took care of the social discussions with neighbors and tended to the details of the children. He had come to realize the heavy burden Priscilla carried as a mother. He always appreciated her warm meals and doting to his every need, and that of Justus and Mary, but he never realized how selfless that was until her passing.

The same as he never knew how much he depended on Khalid for advice, and for the fast way he took care of all the things he delegated him to do. It never occurred to him until his death.

Vitali was a strong reminder of both Khalid and Mary Magdalene. And now he was quickly becoming a reminder of his daughter Mary. Ever since the passing of Khalid, Vitali had attached himself to Mary as her guard and protector.

Death had a way of bringing a person's life full circle and even more so for those who loved them.

Longinus finished securing the supplies to the camel. He had the children mount their horses and he did the same. Longinus firmly tied the leading rein of his camel to his saddle. Ready to ride out, he looked up and saw Arêtes II approaching quickly. He waited.

Arêtes handed Longinus a small parcel wrapped in leather. "Do not open this. When you find Priscilla's brother, give it to him. He will know what to do with it."

Longinus nodded and took the parcel, tucking it inside his shirt. "Thank you for giving us refuge and the provisions needed to travel."

"No need to thank. We are of the same journey. We are one,"

Longinus smiled with appreciation, "Arêtes, this place has shown me many things. My eyes now see - 'what *has been... is ... and yet to be'*, is a circle of one. When completed, all destinies will be fulfilled."

Arêtes, nodded, "A ring of gold, tried in the fire."

Longinus added, "Fanned and flamed by free will."

Arêtes added a warning of caution, "The journey you have been called to take will be filled with deceit. Our Lord warned not to turn our ears away from the truth and listen to myths. Try the spirits always to see what is of God and what is of a lie."

"I have well learned to see and hear such things. The spirit in me is Holy and on that I will trust."

At that, he straightened up in the saddle and nodded at Justus and Mary. "Come. We go now. Follow me."

Arêtes stood and watched as Longinus, Mary, and Justice trotted out of Petra on horseback toward the opening of the sig with Vitali marching close to the side of Mary's horse.

Arêtes II watched until they could no longer be seen. Then quietly he said out loud to himself, "May they find the brother."

"Longinus focused on the sign above the head of the Nazarene pondering the words written in Aramaic, Latin and Greek, "This is Jesus the King of the Jews".

"Longinus set to battle the Djinn."

ABOUT THE AUTHORS

Jon Anthony, Author, is from Washington, Illinois. He is also a recording/sound engineer and has a background as a Music Artist, composer, and song writer. Jon is the keyboard artist, and back up vocalist in the Christian Rock band Glory's Gate. The band has released multiple singles and an album, "Stay Strong". They received the invitational honor to perform at the opening of the Annual Spin Awards in Atlanta, 2018. Glory's Gate music is featured on ITunes, Spotify, Apple, and can also be heard on You Tube. In addition, Jon is the lead singer, guitarist and keyboard artist for his rock band, "The Original Crew".

Dianne Marshall is the author of The Spear of Destiny, Burning Whispers, Sly Foxes, Wolves, and Men, and Manifesting the Wrath. She has been a small business owner for over 30 years, and is dedicated to historical research and writing.
Watch for the future release of Volume one of The Triumphant series titled, "Kuhundra", Co-authored with Jon Anthony.

Ephesians 6:12 KJV
"For we wrestle not against flesh and blood, but against
principalities, against powers, against the rulers of the darkness
of this world, against spiritual wickedness in high places."

CPSIA information can be obtained
at www.ICGtesting.com
Printed in the USA
LVHW020239010221
677984LV00016B/779